BY
TRAVIS LIEBERT

PETRIFYING
ꟼ P
PAGES

Petrifying Pages is a subsidiary imprint of Pure Print Publishing
www.pureprintpublishing.com

CONTENTS

Prologue	6
Prisoner Zero	9
The Little God	17
Bones	29
Beyond the Mask	36
Sins of the Father	42
Art Becomes Him	48
Home Sweet Home	52
The Confession	63
The Grove	67
The Mimic	81
The Dark Web	92
Ghost Town	103
The Terrors of Doctor Marrow	112
The Labyrinth	120
The Greatest Conqueror	133
The Reality Contagion	136
The Oak	156
The Gray King	158
A Correspondence	168
A Note from the Author	181
Acknowledgements	183
About the Author	186

To Jacob and Lilly,
Your support in my endeavors will never be forgotten.
My love for you will never come undone.

Lo: thy dread empire, Chaos, is restored;
Light dies before thy uncreating word:
Thy hand, great Anarch! lets the curtain fall;
And universal darkness buries all.
-Alexander Pope, *The Dunciad*, Line 653

PROLOGUE

In the beginning, there was an anomaly. Some may call Him God, or Allah, or one of the countless other names for the varied and idealistic deities of man. Others may know Him simply as the universe. Some may even go so far as to call Him the Big Bang. All that matters is that He was the prime, the thing that existed before all things, the great force from which all was born.

He was the creator and the destroyer, the sire of order and purveyor of chaos. He reigned above all things, and all things over which He reigned were good. Everything existed as it was meant to be, and every fragment of reality rested in its proper place.

However, after an eternity, the Creator began to change. One would think a being such as Him would be immutable, changeless. But time weighs down upon all. In creating time, He became His own undoing - the child murders the father. His mind fractured and He became a demented shell of what once was.

The inevitability of His decline was not unknown to Him, and it instilled in Him a new state of being, that of terror. For He knew that He would become mindless, unaware of His own actions, incapable of even the simplest thought. He would become an unhinged, omnipotent force. All of reality would be torn apart and sewn back together over and over again, endlessly. Everything and nothing would become one, and all of existence would suffer. Everything He had worked for would come undone.

In the midst of His madness, He decided upon a way to mitigate the destruction brought on by His decline. The Creator shattered himself into countless pieces, an infinite number of aspects, each with a portion of His power. In doing so, reality itself shattered into countless parallels which thus diverged. His parts were all mad - just as He was - nonetheless, He was able to reduce His potential for undoing.

He became The Shattered God, and for eons His aspects laid dormant. However, one by one, they began to wake. They woke angrily, like hibernating animals driven from their slumber. And in time they wrought havoc upon their worlds.

The following stories are a chronicle of this terror, an elegy on the death of order as the Shattered God's aspects all began to rise. What follows is an account of The Undoing and all the chaos that followed.

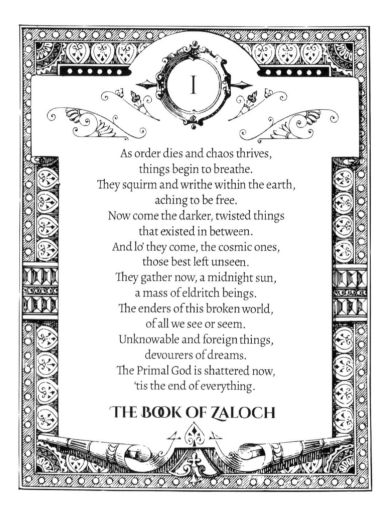

I

As order dies and chaos thrives,
things begin to breathe.
They squirm and writhe within the earth,
aching to be free.
Now come the darker, twisted things
that existed in between.
And lo' they come, the cosmic ones,
those best left unseen.
They gather now, a midnight sun,
a mass of eldritch beings.
The enders of this broken world,
of all we see or seem.
Unknowable and foreign things,
devourers of dreams.
The Primal God is shattered now,
'tis the end of everything.

THE BOOK OF ZALOCH

PRISONER ZERO

He made no attempts to avoid getting caught. The first body was found in a grove of trees near the city park. Soon after, several others were discovered scattered about, haphazardly buried where anyone could find them. Each victim was cut open from throat to groin, then stitched back up and abandoned. His fingerprints and DNA, neither of which appeared in the system, were found at every crime scene. But he had left witnesses who could describe him, and it wasn't long before some city cops came across someone matching the perpetrator's likeness. The evidence confirmed it was him.

During the trial, he pleaded guilty. He didn't even bother getting a lawyer, just represented himself and repeated the same phrase over and over again. "I did what was needed. I buried the seeds."

Everyone figured that by seeds he meant bodies. When asked how many he had buried, he responded, "Twenty-three and one."

After a painstaking search of the city, twenty-three bodies were eventually recovered. The trial dragged on during this period. They never found the extra "one" he always alluded to. But, given his strange wording and precarious mental state, they decided to ignore it and try him for the murder of twenty-three people.

He was sentenced to life without parole. Many argued that he deserved the death penalty for what he did, and there was a great uproar when the verdict was given. His crimes were indiscriminate, emotionless, and methodical. It was the work of someone who was simultaneously deranged and organized.

Nobody knew his real name. He had no identification, no record, and no trace of his existence. He was entered into the prison system as a John Doe. However, a strange system error caused his prisoner number to display as a single zero. It became a joke among the guards. They began to call him Zero, and it wasn't long before his fellow inmates referred to him in the same way. He didn't seem to mind.

Zero was a quiet prisoner. He never resisted when told what to do and never complained about the unsanitary conditions of his cell. Strangely enough, he seemed immune to the predatory nature of the American prison system. None of the other prisoners ever bothered him. Nor did the guards. He remained nonviolent, passive, and self-contained. In many ways, he was the perfect prisoner.

Zero did, however, have one oddity. He would repeat the same phrase over and over again. "I buried the seeds. I buried the seeds. I buried the seeds."

It was a constant monologue that unnerved the guards and inmates alike, but it was always quiet and spoken to himself. It seemed more like a nervous habit than anything malicious. The prison psychiatrist dismissed it as nothing more than a strange fixation, and everyone accepted it as such. Zero lived like that for thirty years. He became one of the oldest inmates in the prison. It seemed he demanded a begrudging respect from those around him, if only for how placid he had remained in his time.

However, one night the other prisoners were woken by a loud cry. Zero's mantra had grown to a frantic wail. Unrelenting, he shrieked about planting the seeds. He lashed and writhed in his cell, and it took five guards to finally restrain him. He was then put in solitary confinement where he later calmed down. For the next several days, Zero's behavior was different. He was less reserved, and he deviated from his typical, repetitive self-talk.

One day, the guards watched as he approached another inmate with a strange swagger to his step. The particular prisoner he approached happened to be a high-ranking member of the Aryan Brotherhood who was a firm believer in violence as a form of conflict management.

"The time is upon us," Zero hissed as he drew uncomfortably close to the other man's face.

The guards instinctively placed their hands on their batons, expecting a fight to break out. To their surprise, the Aryan brother drew away, his tattooed face contorting in an expression of fear and disgust. He stumbled back a few steps, and a look of confusion spread across his face. He seemed baffled as to why he had reacted in the way he did. He turned to confront Zero but stopped dead in his tracks, waved his hand in a gesture of dismissal, and walked away.

The guards glanced at one another in confusion. It seemed the other prisoners were scared of Zero. They thought this strange considering he was nearly in his sixties by then, and even the weakest prisoner there could likely pummel him into the ground. However, their bafflement was only a surface-level reaction. Deep down they could feel it too, the waves of horror that seemed to emanate from the old man. When they looked at him, they felt as if they stood on the edge of a towering cliff, the wind strong at their backs and their lives suspended in the hands of fickle and mysterious gods.

They pretended not to notice it. But the chills that ran down their spines when he passed were undeniable. It was as if there was some abomination lurking within Zero, set to burst forth at any moment and devour all they knew.

During those few days, Zero was put in solitary confinement several times. He never truly did anything to deserve it. While more vocal and perhaps more assertive than before, he wasn't violent and still complied with any orders he was given. The guards put him there simply because they couldn't bear to be in his presence. At least then he was safely out of sight, but not quite out of mind. Somehow, they could still feel him. Whatever emanated from him was like a dark blanket that slowly suffocated the prison.

One day he was particularly outgoing. His disposition could almost be described as giddy. He danced about the prison, eagerly informing his fellow inmates that the time had come, and the seeds would grow.

The guards tried to convince themselves that he was speaking nonsense. It became their own kind of mantra. *It's only nonsense.* After a while, it became a sort of prayer. A strange tension filled the air, as if something large was finally coming to a head. Everyone was on edge that day.

The following night, Zero was oddly quiet. No one heard a peep from his cell. This was unusual considering how vocal he had been as of late. One of the guards was even prompted to investigate, but upon reaching Zero's cell, he felt a strange desire to retreat. A deep wrongness filled the air, and the shadows that enveloped the prisoners' sleeping quarters seemed especially dark that night. He felt that if he stepped into that blackness, he would suffocate in it. He felt that whatever laid beyond the leering darkness would swallow him whole.

He went no further and returned to the guard's quarters, claiming that he had seen nothing strange. The others didn't believe him, but they saw the look on his face and pressed no further. They knew that look well. It was the expression one adopted when living too long in a state of imminent terror. They saw it everywhere, on their fellow guards, on the inmates, and in the mirror every morning.

The next day, a dozen guards stood clustered outside of Zero's cell. One couldn't help but notice the strange perimeter they formed, always keeping a few inches back from the bars. They muttered to one another, hollow words of curiosity that did nothing to mask the fear beneath.

They stared at the thing in Zero's cell. His body was laid precisely in the center of the floor. What could be seen of his skin was dry and sunken, like that of a mummy. Milky, sightless eyes bulged out of his skull and his arms were spread in such a way that he appeared to be some grotesque parody of Jesus on the cross. However, this bizarre display was not what drew the attention of the guards.

A tree sprouted from the dead prisoner's chest. Its wood, if it could be called that, was pitch black and looked as if it had been carved of obsidian. It stood like a gnarled, twisted hand that reached from Zero's very soul, clutching at the world with unending hunger. The guards stared at it, and it seemed the tree stared back. It called to their very bones and drew at them with an unrelenting force. Upon first glance, they knew that to touch the tree was to die and be cast into some nightmarish abyss. They knew it in the same way that one knows fire is hot. They knew it in the same way that they knew the tree could not be allowed to exist.

At first, there were whispers. Then there were shouts as they argued amongst themselves. Next, there was crying. And finally, there was cold, blank acceptance. During all this time, the prisoners had remained unusually quiet. They could feel the blackness that permeated the prison, the horrid thing that stood as a god among their paltry sins by comparison.

The guards began the process of doing what was necessary. It was dark business. It was empty business. Everything was done in grim silence. They gathered the necessary tools. Security footage was turned off, electricity was cut, and they gathered in a mournful cluster around that damned tree.

The gasoline was poured, the match struck, and the prison set ablaze. They felt the weight of the tree's rage at being foiled. They burned in silence, guards and inmates alike. For they knew that everything was happening as it must. Anyone who had been influenced by the tree or Zero in his final days could not be allowed to live. The darkness that had been cast upon the prison would spread like an infection if it wasn't killed completely.

The fire burned hotter and longer than anyone could have rightly guessed. Only the crackle of flames could be heard from the prison's thick walls. But within that crackle, a whispered phrase, "The seeds have grown."

They died silently, neither as heroes nor martyrs, but as victims of something beyond fathom. However, they died knowing that they had succeeded. They thought about how the cursed tree would wither and burn away in the heat of the blaze. They thought about how the terrible truth would die with them.

However, none thought about the twenty-three bodies that had been buried by their grieving families three decades ago. Nor did they consider the rotten black roots that now dug their way into the earth, clutching ever deeper and cementing themselves in the soil. They thought not of the darkness that radiated from those graves nor the plants that began to wilt and die around them. They thought that they had won. And, after the fire had burned long enough, they thought of nothing at all.

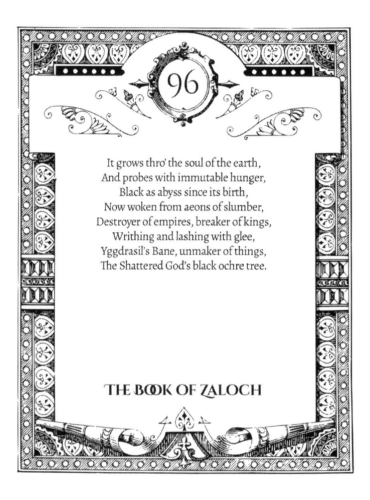

It grows thro' the soul of the earth,
And probes with immutable hunger,
Black as abyss since its birth,
Now woken from aeons of slumber,
Destroyer of empires, breaker of kings,
Writhing and lashing with glee,
Yggdrasil's Bane, unmaker of things,
The Shattered God's black ochre tree.

THE BOOK OF ZALOCH

THE LITTLE GOD

It all began when my parents went out on a date night. They thought I hadn't noticed, but their marriage was struggling, and they were scrambling to fix it. In fifteen years, this was the first time I remembered them ever actually going out on a date. Which meant I was tasked with watching my little brother, Ian.

Most older siblings might bemoan the task of babysitting, but Ian was relatively easy to take care of. He was a quiet and introverted ten-year-old, content to sit still and play video games all day. All I really had to do was make sure he ate and keep him out of trouble.

It was around seven when I heard shouts coming from outside. My friends, Jared and Collin, were out front on their bikes urging me to come hang with them. I checked in on Ian, then - seeing that he was entranced in a video game - headed out the front door. I met my friends on the lawn and we plopped down in the grass.

"What are you doing cooped up inside?" Jared asked.

I nodded back toward the house. "My parents are out on a date night. I'm watching my little brother."

"That blows," Collin said beside me.

I shrugged. "It's not so bad."

Suddenly Jared clapped his hands in excitement. "Oh, I forgot to tell you guys something!"

We waited patiently for him to continue.

"So, my mom was talking to one of the neighbors a couple days ago, and apparently there have been weird lights at the witch house."

I sighed and rubbed my face. "Not this nonsense again."

The witch house was a neighborhood legend my friends had been espousing ever since we were kids. An old decrepit building at the end of our street supposedly housed a witch and was ground zero for a variety of strange phenomena. I believed in the legends for a while but grew out of them as I got older. There was no doubt that someone lived there, but it was likely just a strange, reclusive old lady.

"It's not nonsense," Jared insisted.

"He's right, you know," Collin interjected. "There's a lot of evidence to support the legends."

"It's an urban legend just like any other," I responded. "People have been telling stories about that house for generations. There's nothing special about it."

Jared shot me a smug look. "Then prove it."

"And how exactly do you expect me to do that?"

"Go inside the house and tell us if you see anything strange," he replied.

"What if someone lives there?" I said. "That's breaking and entering. We could get in a lot of trouble."

"Oh please. It's not like anyone's going to call the cops. I doubt that old place even has a landline. Even if they did, the police will just write it off as some kid exploring a local legend. A slap on the wrist at most."

Collin had been watching our exchange in silence but

spoke up. "Jared's right. I don't think anyone would care. Besides, you've been arguing about this for years now. It's about time you nutted up and tried to disprove us."

I ran my hands through my hair in frustration. "Even if I wanted to, I can't." I nodded back toward my house. "I have to watch Ian."

"Aww, is someone a little chicken?" Jared mocked.

Collin looked at me and shrugged. "You know how Jared is. He won't let this go until you do it."

He was right. Jared had a way of annoying people until they did what he wanted, and I was especially susceptible to it. I could wait until my parents got home and then go to the witch house. But by that point it would be late at night, and, despite my disbelief, I didn't find the prospect of going there in the dark very enticing. I could just put it off until another day, but I knew Jared's mocking would only get worse. It was best to get it over with as soon as possible.

"Fine," I said. "But Ian will have to come with us." The other two shrugged. They didn't care. "Give me a minute," I said before going back inside.

I walked to Ian's room where he was still entranced in his video game. "Hey," I said, knocking on the doorframe. "I have to go out for a bit, and you have to come with me."

He continued to play his game, barely acknowledging me with only the barest of glances. "I'll be fine here."

I shook my head. "Mom and Dad would have my ass if anything happened to you while I was gone. I promise it won't take long. I don't want to risk them coming back and finding you alone."

Ian sat in silence for a moment then put his controller down. He got up and walked over to me. "As long as it doesn't take long."

I knew it was stupid to go to the witch house and even stupider to bring my little brother along. But Collin was right. I'd been arguing about this for years and had never actually done anything to disprove their little legend. And besides, I didn't feel like dealing with Jared's mockery for the next several days.

Ian and I walked outside where my two friends waited for me.

"You ready to go?" Jared asked.

I nodded. We began the short walk down the street. It wasn't far, and we found ourselves in front of the house after only a few minutes. The sun hung low above the horizon, bathing the landscape in gold, but that old house always seemed gray. I felt my pulse quicken at the sight of it.

"Okay," Jared said. "We'll wait out here while you take a look inside. Then you can come back and tell us just how normal it is in there. If you don't come back, then we'll assume the worst."

"Wait," I said, holding up my hands. "You guys are supposed to come with me."

"Not my burden to bear." Jared shrugged.

I looked to Collin, but he just shrugged as well. "I'm not going unless I have to."

"Fine," I said. I was already this far. I figured I might as well get it over with. I looked to Ian. "Come on."

Ian shook his head and stepped back. "That house is scary," he said, eyeing the dark structure behind me.

"Mom and Dad said I should keep an eye on you." I wasn't wrong, but deep down I was just afraid to go in that house alone. Despite my arguments, I couldn't help but feel that something terrible loomed inside that building.

"Can't you keep an eye on me from there?"

I shook my head. "Come on Ian. It won't take long."

Ian hesitated for a moment but finally nodded. I began walking up to the house with him close behind. It was easy to see why so many legends had sprouted up around the witch house. It was built long before the other homes in the neighborhood, and its angular gothic style contrasted sharply with the neighborhood's more modern architecture. The lawn was in disrepair, gutters hung loosely from the steep roof, and dirt caked the windows. Nothing about the house indicated habitation, but everyone insisted it wasn't abandoned. Someone owned it and supposedly lived there.

I was embarrassed by the sense of dread I felt when I approached that looming structure. Despite my vehement arguments that it was just a house, something about it inspired fear. I looked over my shoulder at Ian and saw that he was scared too. He gripped my hand tightly and stared at the house, his lip trembling slightly.

As we got closer, I circled around to the backyard. If I was going to break in, it would be best to not be visible from the street. My friends disappeared from sight as I rounded the house. I suddenly felt very alone despite my brother's presence.

Once around back, I searched the house for possible entrances. It was so poorly maintained that I assumed there must be a broken window or door hanging off its hinges somewhere. But it was to no avail. Despite being in disarray, the house seemed unusually secure. Perhaps strange things really did occur in there.

I was rounding to the front of the house with Ian close behind when I nearly tripped over something protruding from the ground. The heavy object was covered in leaves and grass clippings, so I hadn't seen it. I brushed the debris off to find an old cellar door.

It was locked shut, but the padlock was old and heavily rusted. It looked like I could break it. I had Ian stand to the side while I found a fist-sized rock and slammed it against the lock. I winced at the loud clanging it made and worried that someone might hear, but it broke after the next strike, and the cellar door swung open easily.

A gaping darkness greeted me on the other side. I hesitated for a moment then turned to Ian. "You stay here and wait for me, okay?"

I expected him to argue, but, after one look at the dark cellar, he nodded. I breathed a sigh of relief. At least I wouldn't have to deal with him getting lost in the dark or tripping over something and hurting himself. I gingerly climbed down the cellar's rickety stairs, illuminating them with my cellphone's flashlight.

The cellar was damp and reeked of mildew. The stairs creaked loudly beneath my weight as I made my way down. I was surprised by how poorly my flashlight illuminated the room. It was as if the darkness was oppressive, suffocating my light and preventing it from fully revealing what lay within the blackness.

I swept my light around the room, looking for anything *witchy*. I wasn't exactly sure what that encompassed, but I figured I'd know once I saw it. However, after about five minutes I had yet to see anything abnormal. There were old boxes of tools and bags of trash, but nothing occult.

I jumped at the sound of creaking footsteps above. Someone was walking around inside the house. My breathing quickened, and I hurried to examine the rest of the cellar. I should have just left, but the dark room intrigued me.

An eerie atmosphere hung about it. The whole place felt wrong for some reason, and I couldn't help but satiate my curiosity.

Another sound made me nearly drop my phone. This time it came from somewhere in the cellar. It was a strange rocking sound, like a heavy piece of wood being jostled about. I whirled around, trying to find the source of the noise. My light fell upon a strange wooden chest in the corner.

The chest wasn't dissimilar from those you might see in a pirate movie. A latch secured the rounded wooden top onto which was carved a series of intricate, interlocking symbols. Something about those strange runes set me on edge in the same way some people can't bear to hear nails on a chalkboard. Just looking at them made me grind my teeth.

However, what was most unnerving was the fact that the chest was moving. It rocked back and forth as if something inside was struggling to break free. I stepped toward it, but a sudden wave of anxiety forced me to retreat. Something about that box was wrong.

I was about to leave and try to forget about the whole thing when something stopped me in my tracks. The sound of a baby crying emanated from the chest. I slowly turned around and stared at it as the cries went up an octave. A chill went down my spine. Someone was keeping a fucking baby in there.

I instinctively moved to the chest. In hindsight, I should have paid attention to the voice inside me that screamed for me to go away. I should have listened when every fiber of my being resisted my movement toward the box. I should have known that a baby could never rock a heavy chest like that. But the sound of those cries overtook me, and I threw open the lid.

A gust of wind nearly knocked me over. I blinked away the dust that had been kicked up and peered inside the box. There was nothing inside. The chest's interior had the same strange runes as the outside. There were scratches all over the walls, as if something had been scrabbling to get out.

I stepped back, a sudden sick feeling in my gut. I had no idea what had just happened, but for some reason, I was terrified. It felt like something irrevocable had just occurred. A creaking sound behind me sent me whirling.

I turned to see an old woman standing at the foot of the stairs. She wore a simple black outfit. One of her eyes shimmered milky white in the beam of my flashlight, and she blinked in the sudden brightness.

"Who are you?" Her voice sounded husky and ancient.

I tried to respond but the words caught in my throat. She glanced past me at the open chest and her face went white.

"What did you do?" She stepped forward and grabbed me by the collar. "Do you have any idea what you've just unleashed?"

"I- um…." I tried to respond but was too shaken by the sudden turn of events. I didn't even bother trying to pull her hands off me. I felt as if I was in a dream.

"For eons, I've kept that thing locked away. Stars have birthed and died in the time I've been guarding it. And a simpleton like you has gone and unleashed it!" She was shouting by this point and shaking me back and forth. I noticed that she sounded less angry and more scared.

"What was in it?" I asked.

Suddenly her voice dropped to a whisper and she

pulled me close. "The Little God. The most cunning and devious of the elder ones. So much so that his own brothers saw in him the potential for ruin and locked him away. Now he could be anywhere, inside of anybody. He'll grow until he's not so little anymore and burst forth like a butterfly from its cocoon. Then the world will know pain."

I gulped. It all seemed like fantastical nonsense, and yet the fear in her voice was very real. "What do we do?"

"We wait," she said solemnly. "There's nothing else we can do. You've doomed this place and all who inhabit it." The old woman went silent and turned around, then she began to make her way toward the stairs.

Not knowing what else to do, I followed her in grim silence. A terrifying finality hung in the air. I felt like a child who had broken some rule which existed not only for my safety, but for the safety of everything. Something had been let loose.

We ascended the stairs and came out into the open night air. The sun had set, and a full moon cast everything in shades of silver. I hadn't realized how long I'd been down there.

Ian was waiting for me. He stood beside the cellar door in the shadow of the house.

"You two should get going." The old woman sounded defeated. "Try and forget this ev-" her words cut off as she glanced at Ian and I heard her gasp. "It's you," she said.

Ian had always been a cheerful boy, but right then he seemed smug. He glared at the old woman with a look of malice.

"To think you'd inhabit one so close," she said.

"It was convenient," Ian responded. His voice sounded the same, but there was an odd cadence to it. His words carried the assuredness of an eloquent and practiced speaker. Ten-year-old boys didn't speak that way.

The woman glanced toward the cellar and I somehow knew she was thinking about the chest.

"Oh, I'm not going back in there," the thing that was Ian said. He waved his hand in a gesture of dismissal and I heard a loud snap, like a thick branch being broken in half. The old woman collapsed to the ground. "I quite like it here."

Cold sweat ran down my back as I watched the scene unfold before me. It had all happened so fast, so casually, that I barely had time to process it. Ian looked at me, and it seemed his posture changed. He once again seemed like nothing more than a boy.

"Can we go home?" he asked, not even acknowledging the dead woman on the ground. "I'm tired."

I was too stunned to speak, but there didn't seem like anything more I could do. I was scared of him. What would happen if I said no?

I held out my hand and Ian took it. There seemed to be an immense weight to him, as if something greater stood there. We walked hand in hand back to the street. My friends had already left, abandoning me to what I'm sure they imagined to be some terrible fate.

-

It's been six months since that incident. The old woman's death was ruled an accident. Police thought she tripped while walking up the cellar stairs and broke her neck. There was a little buzz around the neighborhood as people mused about how she managed to live there so long while remaining unseen. But no one ever implied there was more to her death.

My friends never spoke of that night again. I suppose they believe I killed that old woman. If only they knew the whole truth.

Ian has been different ever since. He's been assertive in ways children normally aren't. He speaks differently and I notice him manipulating those around him. He's just a boy, after all. However, sometimes he seems much more than a boy. He seems like the thing I saw outside the cellar that night, powerful in a way. At certain moments, when the mood suits him, he seems very much like a little god.

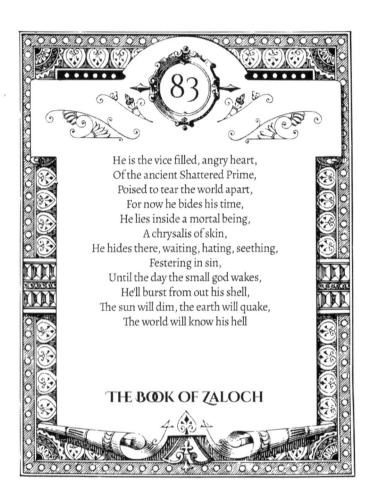

83

He is the vice filled, angry heart,
Of the ancient Shattered Prime,
Poised to tear the world apart,
For now he bides his time,
He lies inside a mortal being,
A chrysalis of skin,
He hides there, waiting, hating, seething,
Festering in sin,
Until the day the small god wakes,
He'll burst from out his shell,
The sun will dim, the earth will quake,
The world will know his hell

THE BOOK OF ZALOCH

BONES

Doctor William Bates was an accomplished and well-respected archaeologist. He had written countless ground-breaking papers, spearheaded the discovery of multiple significant sites, and taught capably. Not only was he well-respected, but he was also well-liked. He regularly appeared as a guest lecturer at nearby universities, and the students he spoke to were always excited to see him.

His personal life thrived as well. He'd recently moved into a new home with his wife and newborn son. All things considered, William Bates lived a good life. He loved his family and he loved his job. He was a happy man. Things were going his way.

That is, until the day he received a strange package. The circumstances of the package's delivery were unusual. It was left on his doorstep in the middle of a Sunday afternoon. The parcel had no indication of a delivery service or a return address. Nobody knocked or rang the doorbell either. He just opened the door one day and it was there.

Perhaps the most perplexing aspect of the package's delivery is the fact it had been delivered at all. William had only just moved into his new house the day before. He had yet to change his mailing address, and only his immediate family knew the location of his new home. Confused by this strange delivery, he brought it inside and opened it.

A letter sat atop a mound of packing foam. It was slightly crumpled and when William unfolded it, he noted that it was written in a shaky script. It was addressed to him but seemed to have been written anonymously. The author claimed to have been an archaeologist who recently embarked on a classified expedition to the arctic circle. Supposedly the expedition team came across a variety of strange specimens, but one, in particular, stood out.

The letter stated that the specimen was contained within the box. The sender claimed it defied all known taxonomical classifications. But this wasn't the reason they had gotten rid of it. The real reason they had sent it to William, the writer claimed, was because of the strange aura that hung about it.

The letter ended rather abruptly and left William more than a little puzzled. He placed it to the side and dug through the box until he came across a wooden case at the bottom. He pulled it out and set it on the table. The seemingly normal briefcase bore no markings.

William opened it to find the specimen carefully tucked in a foam interior, which he removed to examine. He drew in a sharp breath as he looked it over. The specimen was unlike anything he had seen before.

It appeared to be the spinal structure of some organism. A central column ran down the middle while sharp, rib-like projections jutted from the sides. The central column transitioned into what appeared to be a tail made from countless tiny interlocking bones which ended in a sharp point, much like that of a stingray.

He immediately noticed that the structure was very different from that of most fossils. While fossils may often appear bonelike, they are actually comprised of sediments compacted in the shape of whatever creature became trapped in them. But William noticed that this fossil appeared to be made of actual bone. It showed none of the decay or sedimentation that typical fossils exhibit. He briefly wondered if it was actually some ancient specimen or merely a recently deceased species. Before he could spend any time musing on the age of the specimen, he noticed something even more intriguing about it.

The fossil, if one could call it that, had an unusual pattern to it. Silver lines spiraled down the length of each bone and they glimmered strangely in the light. William thought it might have been a trick, some added decoration, but as he examined the specimen more closely, he saw there were grooves in the bones where the composition differed. It was these grooves that shone in the light. Perhaps someone had etched them there, but he could find no evidence of any tool use on the bones. They were in perfect condition.

William was fascinated by the strange fossil and rambled on about it to his wife all night. He decided to take it to the local university and use their equipment to examine it more closely the next day. That night he dreamt of the specimen and its beauty.

He spent the entirety of the next day using various tools and methods to examine the fossil. His colleagues were amazed by it and mused as to what kind of person could have sent it to him. All of the tests indicated that the specimen wasn't fake. And, the more they researched it, the more baffled they became.

Using carbon dating they were able to determine that it was Pre-Cambrian. However, most of William's colleagues cast doubts upon the accuracy of that date as only unicellular organisms existed then. William argued that the date was accurate and that the specimen represented a breakthrough in how the evolutionary timeline should be perceived. He had a strange habit of referencing the specimen's beauty when making these arguments, as if that somehow made them more reputable.

They were also able to determine the composition of the strange silver spirals that ran along the specimen. Grooves ran down each bone, and each of those grooves was filled with mercury, which was then sealed by a thin, translucent carbon-based structure to keep it contained. It was this discovery that had the scientists most excited. Mercury is highly toxic and a multicellular creature that somehow integrated it into its bones seemed practically impossible.

William's colleagues wanted to keep the specimen in the lab overnight in order to further study it, but he insisted on bringing it home with him. He began to ramble about how he didn't want its beauty tainted but caught himself and left in silence. His colleagues shot him strange glances as he left.

When he came home, he spoke only of the specimen all evening. His wife was happy to see him so excited about a potential scientific breakthrough but noted that he almost seemed infatuated with the thing. He spoke of it in strangely familiar terms, at one point even insinuating that the specimen found him of its own accord. She felt a sense of unease when she saw William place the fossil on his nightstand before going to bed but chose to say nothing.

She was roused several hours later by the sound of the baby crying in the next room. She got up to calm him and noticed that William wasn't in bed beside her. For a moment, she thought that he'd gotten up to take care of the baby, but then she noticed him sitting in a chair in the corner of the room. He was just barely visible in the silver moonlight. He sat there with the fossil in his hands, turning it over and over as he stared at it. The sight sent chills down her spine.

She almost said something but chose not to for reasons she didn't understand. Instead, she silently left the room to take care of their child. She returned thirty minutes later after changing him and rocking him to sleep only to find that her husband hadn't moved from the corner. Unnerved, she returned to bed and tried to get back to sleep. As she drifted off, she thought she heard William whispering to the thing in his hands.

He carried the specimen with him throughout the entirety of the next day. Just like before, he spoke of it constantly, but soon the topic of conversation changed. He began to muse on how beautiful bones in general were. He claimed that the new fossil had made him realize the inherent beauty in bones. He went on and on about how all bones had beauty to them. That they were works of art.

Several days later packages started arriving in droves at the Bates house. William excitedly answered the door whenever one came and tore open the packaging as soon as he was back inside. Each one was a new collection of bones. He had begun to order them online and couldn't seem to stop. They were all so beautiful, every intricate curve so enticing.

Over the next several weeks, William's collection of bones grew and grew until they filled every corner of his office. They soon spilled out into the hallway until the house was littered with boxes of old bones and fossils. He spent and spent until all of their savings were gone. This led to fights between William and his wife, but each time he remained completely placid and explained that the bones were too beautiful to pass up. It seemed he genuinely couldn't understand why his wife didn't understand his obsession.

One night, William was turning the specimen over and over in his hands as he often did, watching it shimmer in the light. It had a calming effect on him. It was almost hypnotic in a way. He was contemplating the wondrous beauty of bones when he came upon a realization. He had never actually seen a bone in its natural state. That is, he had never seen one inside of a living body. All of the bones he had were dead. The idea haunted him. If something could be so enticing as a desiccated remnant of the past, he couldn't imagine what it must be like as a natural, living structure.

He tried to put it out of his mind, but the thought kept coming back. He just couldn't get it out of his head. He realized that it was something he needed to see. There was no avoiding it. Such things just had to be seen for oneself. He felt as if he was in a dream and everything he did next was enveloped in some strange haze.

He soon found himself upstairs in the bedroom. It wasn't hard to pin his wife down and tie her up. He was a large man. With that done, he shoved an old rag in her mouth. The screaming annoyed him and would distract him from his task. Then he began the cutting. At first, it was just messy, but once the bones were revealed it became glorious. There they sat in their natural cavities surrounded by flowing blood. His eyes welled up at the beautiful sight.

He cut and cut, revealing every bone. But he became too excited and stopped being careful. It wasn't long before the screaming and the struggling stopped. The blood stopped flowing and the bones lost much of their luster.

Unsatisfied, William moved to the room next door.

BEYOND THE MASK

The man in the mask has lived for many years. More than anyone else to his knowledge, though, it was not a topic he entertained often. He had no name, for it had been lost over the years, and names mattered not to one such as him. He escaped names and likewise, he escaped definition. To pin him down with words would be impossible, but for now, he shall be known by what he appears to be: the man in the mask.

The man had neither friends nor acquaintances. Similarly, he had neither family nor lovers, for he existed at the edge of people's awareness and perceptions. They might make way for him on a busy sidewalk or absentmindedly hold a door for him, but they would not recall doing so, nor would they remember that there had been a man at all.

Children, however, were different. Perhaps they were more conscious than their adult counterparts, or perhaps they were simply more intrigued by those barely perceptible things at the edges of their vision. The reasons for this difference were irrelevant. What mattered was that children would notice the man in the mask more often than not. Their gazes followed him, and sometimes they would point, tugging at their mother's blouse and directing her attention to the strange figure. Of course, her gaze would slide right over him, and she would ignore their outburst. Eventually, the child would become bored or their ability to perceive the man would deteriorate, and they too would forget he had ever been there.

That was the way things had been ever since the man in the mask could remember. He had always drifted just outside of human consciousness and consequently existed at the furthest extremes of reality, the outskirts of what the human mind knows to be real. So it went, as one day blurred into the next so the man blurred into the world around him. However, all that changed the day he met Billy.

Billy seemed to be an ordinary child of no more than ten. He enjoyed the things that most little boys do: action figures, playing outdoors, getting dirty. He was also friendly and insatiably curious. Which is why, when he saw the man in the mask, he decided to say hi.

This may seem like an ordinary course of action, and one might assume that this was merely a side effect of Billy's outgoing personality. But for the man, this was beyond belief. Never had anyone spoken to him. The thought had never even crossed anyone's mind. He was a fleeting dream, an entity that resisted comprehension and defied even the notion of communication.

That is why when young Billy greeted him with an enthusiastic grin, the man in the mask was, for the first time in his existence, surprised. He had no response for this pure and wholesome act of childhood. He only stood stock-still, staring down at the boy through the eyes of his plain mask, beautiful in its simplicity. The man did not respond, for language was of no use to him and he had forgotten what it was to speak ages ago. Then, for no reason that he could think of, he waved at the boy.

Billy giggled, a high-pitched sound that made the man's eyes widen. Surely, he had heard children laugh countless times in the course of his existence, but those sounds had faded away from his awareness like all others, mere phantoms of a world that he was no longer part of.

"You're funny," Billy said, staring at the man, surely intrigued by his odd manner and attire.

The man didn't know how to respond, so he merely nodded. Billy grinned even wider at the man's simple acknowledgement. Suddenly, a voice rang out from near-by. Billy's mother called his name, and with it a slew of threats if he didn't find his way back to her immediately. Spurred by his mother's call, Billy ran in the direction of the voice, sparing the man a wave as he did so.

The man watched Billy go, intrigued for the first time in memory.

Driven by this intrigue, the man followed Billy home. He found that the boy lived in an insignificant house on an insignificant lane in some insignificant part of a city whose name the man in the mask had long forgotten or never knew in the first place.

For several days the man simply watched. He saw the boy coming to and from school, playing in his yard, and even stayed well into the night as the light in Billy's room finally went out and the neighborhood lay in silence.

The man in the mask had never needed to hide before, and so it was an act that did not come naturally to him. The idea of needing to be out of sight to remain unseen was a foreign thought. Nonetheless, he managed to avoid Billy's notice for those first few days.

It wasn't until the fourth day that Billy became aware of the man. Billy played outside, wielding an old branch like a sword, surely imagining himself as some pirate or knight, when he turned to see the man lurking at the edge of the lawn.

Billy's face lit up with an unexpected smile. "Hi, Mister Mask."

The man stood still for a moment, pondering what the child had just said. Mister Mask. A sensible name. He nodded almost imperceptibly with approval then raised his hand and waved at the boy. Despite the impedance of his mask, he hoped that Billy could tell that, for the first time ever, he was smiling.

That day began the strangest of relationships. The man, henceforth known as Mister Mask, remained mute, but he managed to communicate with Billy through simple gestures. The boy enthusiastically accepted Mister Mask's odd mannerisms and even seemed to enjoy them. And so they played on and on. Simple games that similarly require simple communication. Things such as hide-and-seek or tag.

Billy's parents assumed that the boy had created an imaginary friend and dismissed it just as easily. Even if they had suspected anything, Mister Mask's existence would have slipped from their memory almost as soon as the thought came into their heads. Over the course of several years, Billy and Mister Mask developed a deep bond, made strong by its simplicity and purity.

Among these many firsts, Mister Mask had a much more surprising one. For the first time in his existence, he felt love.

By the time Billy was thirteen, he interacted with Mister Mask every day. Their relationship was a simple one. Mister Mask kept Billy company, listened when he needed to talk, and played when he needed to play.

Then came one fateful day when the pair were playing tag. Billy had grown tall and the top of his head just cleared Mister Mask's chin. As Billy sprinted after him in the midst of the game, Mister Mask attempted to deftly avoid his outstretched arm. But when Billy got close, his feet became tangled beneath him and he tripped over himself. As he fell, the top of Billy's head cracked against his playmate's mask and sent it tumbling to the ground.

Billy laid there in the cool, wet grass as he stared up into the face of Mister Mask. He was stunned for a moment, and he blinked until his vision cleared. His companion's ancient visage came into sharp focus. In that face, he saw the truth of things, the obscene reality that exists beyond our own.

The man killed him quickly and silently. Any longer staring into the lines that eternity had etched on his face, and Billy would end up just like him. That was not an existence he wanted for the boy.

He paused for a moment and stared down at the dead boy's body. Billy seemed peaceful, like an angel upon fresh spring grass -an angel that had learned too much of the way of things.

Having had his moment, the man in the mask stepped over the dead boy and returned to his existence at the edge of all we know.

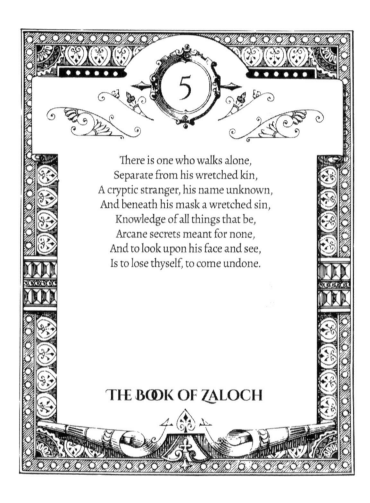

5

There is one who walks alone,
Separate from his wretched kin,
A cryptic stranger, his name unknown,
And beneath his mask a wretched sin,
Knowledge of all things that be,
Arcane secrets meant for none,
And to look upon his face and see,
Is to lose thyself, to come undone.

THE BOOK OF ZALOCH

SINS OF THE FATHER

Doctor James Masters showed a new patient into his office. The young man seemed nervous. His eyes darted about the room and he took slow steps. He appeared unsure of how to situate himself until Masters gestured to a couch that sat across from his desk and shot the man a reassuring smile. It was common for patients to be uncomfortable, especially at their first time in therapy. However, he had been a psychiatrist for years and was adept at putting people at ease.

Masters sat across from his patient and smiled at him once again. In response, the young man gave him a tight-lipped smile which bordered on a grimace.

"It's nice to meet you, Harry." Doctor Masters said. "How are you today?"

There was an awkward moment of silence before Harry responded. "I'm okay, I suppose. Not really better than usual, but not much worse either."

"I see," Masters said nodding. "I already have a general idea from the survey you filled out, but I'd like for you to tell me in your own words what brings you here."

Harry chewed his lip thoughtfully. "Well, I guess I've been feeling down. Everything seems exhausting and boring to me. I don't really like life so much anymore."

The Doctor nodded once again and jotted something down on the notepad in front of him. "And are their any other feelings that accompany this sensation of being down?"

"I get this weird tight feeling in my chest sometimes. It's like I'm scared but not of anything in particular. I just know something bad is going to happen. It's especially bad in public. Whenever I'm around people I start to feel all tight and shaky, and it's like I'm breathing through a coffee straw."

"So, you would say that anxiety seems to be a significant problem?"

"Yeah," Harry responded simply.

"That's fairly common in those that experience symptoms of depression as well. The two tend to go hand in hand." Masters explained. "Typically, one tends to be the root cause which creates the other. For example, one may become depressed because their social anxiety prevents them from going out and they feel lonely." He watched Harry closely to ensure he was listening to the explanation. His patient seemed a little absent, as if he was only half paying attention to everything around him. This behavior seemed odd. Based on Harry's description of his symptoms, one would expect him to be hypervigilant around others.

"Do you have any idea which one could be the root cause? Does the depression or anxiety seem more prevalent?"

Harry shrugged. "I dunno, isn't it kind of your job to figure that out."

Doctor Masters gave him a wry smile. "I suppose it is, but this is a team effort. We need to work together if

I'm to help you and that means conveying how you feel to me."

"I guess that makes sense," Harry said. "I suppose the anxiety is the worst. I always feel like I'm running out of time."

"What do you mean you're running out of time?" Masters inquired.

"I've got something big and important to do, but I always feel like I'm behind schedule and it'll never get done."

"What important thing do you have to do, Harry?"

The young man began to fidget with a ring he wore on his right hand. Doctor Masters hadn't noticed it until then. It seemed like an odd statement piece, the kind of thing you might see a rebellious teenager wear. It was thick and made of stone. The bottom was smooth, but the top consisted of a series of spikes projected up the entire length of his finger. Harry seemed to relax as he twirled the fiddled with the ring.

"Is there something you have to do?" The doctor prompted.

"Yes," Harry said. His voice had taken on a sterner tone. It contained none of the uncertainty that Masters had noticed before.

"And what task is that?"

"I have to kill my father." He said.

Masters was taken aback. "Why do you have to kill your father?"

"He did a bad thing," Harry said. He sounded like a completely different person now. There was a confidence about him. It was almost snide.

"What bad thing did he do?"

Harry looked up at the doctor. His eyes were cold and

unblinking.

"Twenty-three years ago, my father met a girl. She was only fifteen years old, but she'd snuck into a bar, which is where she ran into him. He was traveling and, after getting her sufficiently drunk, took her back to his motel."

Doctor Masters' eyes grew wide as Harry recounted his story.

"He tried to have sex with her, but she resisted. That was when he got angry. He beat her senseless. She suffered three broken bones and a major concussion. While she was unconscious, he raped her at least four times then disappeared without a trace. No one knew who he was, and he had paid for the motel in cash. The woman was found in a comatose state the next day when cleaning services came into the room."

Masters listened to the story calmly, but something dark moved behind his eyes. Harry was still staring directly at him. He had yet to blink.

"That woman was taken to a hospital where she remained in a coma. It wasn't until three weeks later that the staff realized she was pregnant. She remained unconscious for the entire duration of the pregnancy. After nine months she finally went into labor. The stress of it was too much on her body and she died during childbirth."

"And what of the child?" Masters asked. His voice was hurried, anxious like Harry's had been when he first entered. There was an intense curiosity behind his eyes. But there was also something deeper, something like fear.

"They performed an emergency C-section and managed to save the boy," Harry said. "He grew up in the foster care system where he was subjected to countless horrors: violence, hunger, molestation. He had no respite from the terrors of an uncaring system."

Masters was tense now. He watched Harry carefully, eyeing every movement. Unbeknownst to his patient, the Doctor gripped a sharp letter opener beneath his desk.

"And what of the boy now?" Doctor Masters probed.

"He found his father," Harry said with a smirk. Without warning, he stood up and began to pace the room. He had removed the ring from his finger and now fiddled with it, tossing it from hand to hand. The doctor's grip on the letter opener tightened.

"How did you find me?" Masters said. Harry continued to fiddle with his ring as he walked in slow, measured circles.

"There's a certain irony in being born from a dead body. In a way, it was more like I was exhumed than born. A certain change occurs in the darkness of a dead womb. I became touched by something in there, something cold and ancient. Briefly, I existed in two different worlds. And the remnants of that second world hung about me like a cloak for the rest of my life. This cloak can become a tool if one is open to the darkness within and without."

Harry stopped and gazed at the ring in his hand. There was a longing in his eyes.

"I was guided by one of them, the mad and virulent aspects of the broken one. He sensed my lust for pain, and it drew him to me. He forged me into his weapon and directed me to you." At that, Harry pointed at Doctor Masters.

"The time is upon us, *father*." He enunciated the last word quietly, but it carried a certain weight behind it, twenty-two years of hatred and pain.

Doctor Masters lurched forward with the letter opener, but Harry caught his arm. The doctor felt his bones shatter as Harry squeezed. His strength was inhuman.

With surgical precision, he reached forward and drove the pointed end of his ring into his father's eye. The doctor gasped in pain and stumbled back. He collapsed on the desk and uttered a wretched sound. He clutched at his eye and writhed until his screaming became a low moan then faded to nothing at all.

Doctor Masters sat stock-still and stared through the ring that now occupied his eye socket. It hadn't pierced his eyeball but rather was the perfect size to encircle it. A look of terror came across the doctor's face, but he could force no sound from his mouth.

"Now you see His truth. You belong to Him now, the one who brought me to you." Harry crouched before the seemingly frozen doctor. "You'll be in this state for the rest of your life. Everyone will think you're in a coma. But you'll still be in there, completely aware. And He will show you all the horrors of this world and the ones beyond. You will writhe in agony at all He shows you, but your pain will be His ecstasy."

Harry left the room in silence while his father sat and saw all things unfit for human sight.

ART BECOMES HIM

Thomas sat before a blank canvas, paintbrush in hand, and desperately tried to think of something, anything, to paint. He had been at this for three days now, just staring at the endless field of white that haunted him. His apartment was in disarray, much like his thoughts.

Things had gone terribly for him ever since he decided to move out on his own and pursue a career in art. He knew it would be difficult. Hell, he figured it might even be impossible. But he never could have foreseen things going this poorly.

Rent was due in four days, his bank account was overdrawn, and it had been months since anyone expressed interest in buying one of his pieces. His stomach growled, reminding him of his empty fridge and pantry.

His only option was to paint something good for once. To make a piece that would sell without fail and at least earn him enough to make this month's rent. But if that was to be the case, then this piece would have to be greater than any of his previous works. It would have to be inspired. Some divine masterpiece beyond what he could normally create.

At that moment, as if the universe responded to some

silent command, Thomas felt something overtake him. An idea of sorts, but so much more. It wasn't concrete. The strange sensation was more like a call to action, a desperate need to follow this vague blueprint which had appeared in his head.

Gripped by this need, he began to paint. There was neither thought nor planning to his art. Only action. He painted without really seeing, each stroke guided by something beyond him. This divine force drew his brush across the canvas in a frenzy of blacks and grays with hidden depths of crimson. It was jumbled chaos. It was nonsense. It was beautiful.

But this wasn't the end. Thomas continued painting on and on, filling one canvas then moving to the next. There was no pausing to appreciate or observe. After all, there was no need to do so. The force that held him was perfect, and its creation would be perfect too.

He felt the pangs of hunger in his stomach. It had been days since he'd last eaten, and by that point, he had been working on his magnum opus for hours. But there was no stopping him. He ignored the pain, or perhaps he never felt it in the first place. For Thomas was no longer there in a sense. He had left himself and become a tool of something greater.

Eventually, he ran out of canvases. Many would have stopped at least long enough to get new supplies. But not Thomas. Without even taking a breath, he moved seamlessly from the canvas to the walls of his apartment. Deep down he was aware that he shouldn't be painting on the walls, but he was driven and knew that stopping for even the briefest of moments would break the spell.

He moved from wall to wall, filling each one up as quickly and smoothly as the last. And when he ran out of wall space, he moved to the floors, and then to the objects that laid scattered about the small room. Furniture, appliances, clothes, and windows. Everything was subject to his grand vision.

Eventually, he ran out of things to paint. Every inch of every surface in the apartment was covered in fragments of his creation like some glorious puzzle. It was at that point that he paused for a moment. What to do next? He couldn't stop. He could feel that things were not yet finished. There was still work to be done.

After only the briefest of pauses, he stripped off his clothing and began to paint on himself. He would become his work. His greatest piece. A tribute to the higher power that guided him. And as he felt the cold paint spread across his body, his master's voice began to speak.

Yes, my child. You have only painted a fragment of my essence into existence. But that is all that is needed for now.

Spurred by the voice of his master, Thomas's painting became frantic. His brushstrokes became great swirls of color across his body until his skin was a myriad of dark shades. He felt the paint enter his mouth, then his nose, then an iciness as it was drawn across his eyes like a veil.

We are one now, my acolyte. You have made me incarnate. Together we shall paint the world in our righteous colors.

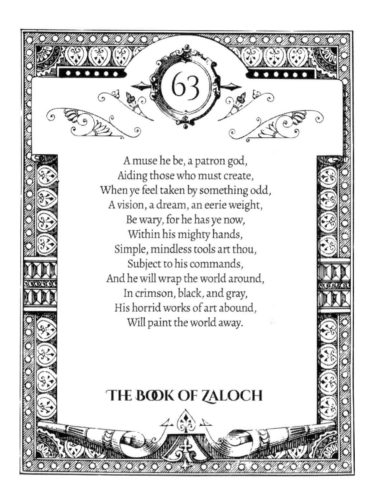

63

A muse he be, a patron god,
Aiding those who must create,
When ye feel taken by something odd,
A vision, a dream, an eerie weight,
Be wary, for he has ye now,
Within his mighty hands,
Simple, mindless tools art thou,
Subject to his commands,
And he will wrap the world around,
In crimson, black, and gray,
His horrid works of art abound,
Will paint the world away.

THE BOOK OF ZALOCH

HOME SWEET HOME

Theresa sighed as she carried the last of her boxes into the house. It was difficult to navigate around the swell of her belly. She set the box down and smiled as she felt the baby kick. It wouldn't be long before he was due. The past eight months had flown by, but then again there had been so much going on.

Theresa thought about the baby's father, Patrick. No one knew where he was. He had disappeared only a few short days after the pregnancy announcement. He took only his wallet, his phone, and some clothes. She should have known he wouldn't stick around. She had seen the look on his face when he found out she was pregnant, the intense anxiety, the complete absence of any love or care. Yet she had believed he would change once he'd become accustomed to the truth. She sighed at how naïve she'd been.

And then there was the matter of her own father. Everyone had known that he wouldn't beat stage four prostate cancer, but no one had expected just how quickly he would go. She hoped that perhaps he had been reunited with her mother. She smiled grimly at the thought. Theresa had rejected the idea of religion years ago, but deep down she still hoped that there was happiness at the end of it all. At the very least, she hoped there was something more than darkness.

Now it was just her. She stared at the old Victorian house she'd bought with the money her father left her. It was old and dusty, but still she couldn't believe how cheap it had been considering its size. The realtor had seemed unusually eager to be rid of it. Theresa couldn't understand why. The house wasn't pristine, but it was decent and perfectly livable. At least she would have a home to raise the baby in. It was nice and secluded, far away from the dangerous and disappointing world she knew all too well.

She slowly unpacked her things. There was barely enough to fill an apartment - let alone a six-bedroom home. Most of her belongings were sequestered away in the master bedroom, while kitchen supplies and toiletries went in their respective places. Once that was done, she noted that the house would require a thorough cleaning. No one had lived there in a long time, and a layer of grime had settled over everything. Theresa decided to save the cleaning for later. She was exhausted from the move. Silently, she chided herself for not hiring someone to help her. Independence wasn't always a virtue.

Theresa decided to relax and simply wander the rooms of the house. It was nothing she hadn't seen before, but it was nice to take it all in and know that it now belonged to her and the baby. As she moved about, she noticed something strange about her new home. It was completely silent. There were none of the odd creaks and pops that you would expect in an old building. Even her footsteps were oddly muffled. It somehow felt as if the house was watching with bated breath, waiting for something to happen.

That strange thought sent shivers down her spine. She tried to ignore the realization. Still, the silence continued. It pressed against Theresa like a great weight, slowing her movements and exhausting her. Feeling drained by the drowsy quietude of her new home, she went to bed early and slept soundly through the night.

When she woke up the next day, the silence was gone. It was as if the house had seen what it was watching for and was now abuzz with excitement. Floors creaked and popped, stairs groaned, and the entire house shivered with movement. Theresa noticed the change, but it was soon put out of her mind as she busied herself with organizing her belongings.

She spent much of the day putting things in their proper places. Later, she went out for groceries and returned to find the house as it had been, alive with sounds and drafty breezes as all old homes should be. Still, it seemed that an odd energy filled the air, as if life had been breathed into the structure itself.

Theresa was dimly aware of this throughout the day but ignored it. She spent much of the evening browsing through a book of potential baby names. She knew the baby was a boy but had yet to choose a name for him. She mused on how Patrick should have been there helping her. The thought left a bitter taste in her mouth.

Deciding she was done looking at names, Theresa turned off all the lights in the house and went to bed. The master bedroom was a large, open space, and she realized just how small and alone she felt within it. She placed her hands on the swell of her belly and reminded herself that she was never truly alone.

Later that night something woke her. Theresa groggily rubbed her eyes and listened intently. A noise came from nearby. It sounded like someone was whispering faintly. As she listened, it grew louder.

"A baby," the voice hissed. "At last we have a baby once again."

She couldn't determine where the sound was coming from. One moment it came from the hallway, and the next it came from the darkness of the vaulted ceiling, only to emanate from the bathroom mere seconds later. The voice bounced around her from room to room, corner to corner, shadow to shadow.

"I'm so excited," said the voice. "How I've longed for a baby of my own." As it spoke it faded until those last words were just barely audible.

Theresa, still groggy, fell back asleep and hardly remembered the event in the morning. All she recalled was a vague sense of unease stemming from the night before. If she thought about it, she might have remembered hearing some disembodied discussion of her child, but deep down she didn't want to remember. Some things were better left forgotten. To forget is to dull the blade of the past so that it can no longer hurt you. To lie to oneself is a survival mechanism.

The next day she noticed just how large her belly had gotten. The baby would likely be here any day now. Despite the state of her pregnancy, she was determined to work on cleaning the house. The baby should come back to a clean and healthy home.

She decided to start with the large windows upstairs which overlooked the foyer. They had accumulated dust over the years and light was barely able to penetrate them, and the little light that did seemed to cast a sickly glow upon everything it touched. As she made her way up the stairs, she noticed a loose board that stuck out and nearly caught the bottom of her dress. That would need to be fixed at some point. Someone might trip and get hurt.

The windows were more than twice as tall as her, and she ended up having to tape her duster to the end of a broom before she could reach them in their entirety. Eight arched panes of glass lined the upstairs balcony and continued down an adjoining hallway. Theresa hummed as she made her way down the row of windows.

She had dusted half the windows when she thought she heard voices coming from nearby. She stopped and listened intently. Her heart pounded in her chest. It sounded like an argument was taking place in hushed tones. She briefly wondered if someone was in the house.

The argument seemed to emanate from an empty bedroom down the hall. She considered calling the police, but the voices beckoned to her. She wanted to hear what they were saying. She couldn't quite put her finger on it, but there was something strangely enticing about the ghostly conversation.

The door to the bedroom was tightly shut. She pressed her ear up against it and listened closely. Her eyes widened at what she heard. It wasn't an argument, but rather someone angrily ranting to themselves.

"A bad mother is what she is," the voice hissed. "She has no idea what she's doing. She'll kill the baby before I ever get a chance to love it."

Theresa could hear the sound of footsteps pacing back and forth on the other side of the door. The voice moved round and round as it mumbled on about how bad a mother she was.

"That woman has no business carrying a child. She doesn't eat right, and she doesn't care for it. I won't have it. It should be *my* child, not hers."

A floorboard creaked beneath Theresa's weight and both the voice and footsteps came to a sudden stop. She waited for the voice to say more, but only silence remained on the other side. After what seemed like an eternity, she opened the door.

The bedroom was empty. There was nothing on the other side save a barren floor covered with layers of dust. Theresa examined the floor for footprints, but there were none. The room had been completely undisturbed for a while now.

A sense of nausea began to swell in her gut as she paced around the empty room. It was completely open and empty. There was nowhere to hide. Cold chills made their way down her spine and she clutched her belly. Everything about the house suddenly felt wrong.

The queasy feeling stayed with her long after she left the room. After the incident, she couldn't work up the energy to do any more cleaning. She just tried to relax and calm herself. The creaks and pops of the old home suddenly sounded very different. They were no longer lively and exciting, but rather threatening. It seemed as if the house was a very different place than before. She felt very small in the bowels of that great structure.

That night a strange noise roused Theresa, and she woke to find her bedroom drenched in a sickly red light. Incomprehensible voices whispered around her. They gargled in tongues unknown to man and the horrible, bubbling, twisted sounds that emanated from the shadows set her heart racing. Somehow, she knew they were talking about her baby.

Just then the room's lighting turned a darker shade of crimson. A voice came from the darkness of the vaulted roof above her.

"That baby is mine," it hissed. "You don't deserve it."

Theresa screamed and tried to run, but she couldn't move. It was as if her arms were pinned to the bed. She writhed but to no avail. A great weight sat upon her, pressing her into the sheets until she could barely breathe. She took ragged, shuddering breaths that never quite reached her lungs and felt as if she would suffocate.

Just then, black tendrils descended from the darkness above. Theresa screamed again, but there was no one to hear, only the horror that dwelled within her house. The tentacle-like shadows began to feel about her body. They were almost gentle in the way they touched her, caressing the swell of her stomach. Then, as if prompted by some invisible signal, they began to tear at her. Her belly split and crimson gore splattered across the sheets. They ripped the baby from her womb, and she watched helplessly as the screaming, bloody child was carried up into the darkness of the rafters.

Theresa woke from the nightmare with a start. Her hands instinctively went to her belly where she found the baby safe and her body intact. She began to cry then. It was all too much for her. It felt like her life was falling apart. First, she found herself pregnant and alone, and now she was being plagued by phantom voices and nightmares. It was too much. Theresa spent much of that night crying only to drift off for a couple hours of fitful sleep.

She woke up feeling groggy and sick the next day. The terrors of the night before hung about her like a cloak and weighed heavily upon her. She mostly laid in bed but began to feel restless in the afternoon. Eventually, she decided to get up and do something. As if urging her to act, she felt the baby kicking within her.

Theresa made her way from the bedroom and meandered through the house, absentmindedly searching for some kind of task to keep her attention. She couldn't seem to find anything to do when suddenly she remembered that she had left the upstairs windows unfinished. She gathered her cleaning supplies and slowly plodded her way up the stairs.

Everything was as she had left it. Half of the windows were still dirty and the door to the bedroom from which she had previously heard voices was tightly closed once again. She breathed a sigh of relief at that. Maybe things weren't so bad after all. She just needed to fall into some kind of routine, and then maybe the house would begin to feel like home.

She began cleaning as she had the day before. Theresa still felt clouded by a dense fog and couldn't quite shake it. However, she managed to fall into a rhythm, though she remained acutely aware of the nauseous sensation that hung about her. She considered going to see a doctor but decided she was just tired.

Theresa methodically made her way down the row of windows. As she did so, more and more light spilled into the house. It began to feel like a warm and welcoming place. The cold draftiness of the old Victorian structure was steadily being replaced by a warm and modern livelihood. Theresa smiled at that, though it didn't quite reach her eyes.

She had just gotten to the last window at the end of the hallway when she felt a slight popping sensation. She looked down to notice a trickle of water running between her legs.

"Shit," she said. Her water had broken. She needed to get to the hospital.

Just then, a sudden change came over the house. A buzzing sound filled the air, like that of an electric current. The entire structure shuddered, and her surroundings grew ice cold. The light that had only just begun to spill through the clean windows turned a sickly gray, and the shadows it cast took on a new depth.

"My baby," Theresa heard a voice whisper right behind her ear. She whirled around to find nobody there. She shook her head and tried to focus on getting downstairs and out to her car. This was no time to be spooked by an old house.

She turned around and gasped. The hallway before her seemed impossibly long and the stairs were but a speck in the distance. She tried to blink away the illusion, but it remained. Now terrified, Theresa began to make her way down the hall, moving as fast as she could while still being mindful of the baby. Water dripped from between her legs as she moved in an awkward waddling gait.

The stairs seemed to grow closer as she moved forward, but much more slowly than they should have. It was as if she was moving in slow motion, her destination approaching only at a tenth of the rate at which she moved. The carpet began to come up in strange humps and folds as if something writhed beneath it. The sudden motion threatened to trip her, and she had the distinct sense that the house was trying to make her fall.

She stepped carefully around the obstacles and tried to focus on her destination. Her breathing was labored, and her heart felt like it was going to pop. There was so much going on. Everything seemed wrong. She just wanted to be out of that damned house.

She walked and walked, and slowly but surely the stairs crept ever closer. She was nearly there when a nearby movement caught her attention. The wood-paneled wall beside her warped and bulged. It sunk outward like a balloon filling with water and a simple eyeless imitation of a face began to form in front of her. The wood groaned and expanded until it looked like a pregnant woman had been incorporated into the wall. Its belly twisted and writhed as if something was moving inside of it, and two small handprints pressed out of the swell.

"Mommy," a child's voice said from the wall. "Let me go. This is where I belong."

Theresa gasped and covered her mouth with her hands. As she stepped back, she nearly tripped over another of those strange warps in the carpet.

"Don't you want what's best for me, mommy?"

She shook her head and tried to respond but no words came. The air left her lungs and a dimness hung about the edges of her vision. Theresa felt like she was suffocating. Desperate to get away, she turned and blindly ran down the hall. As she ran, she began to feel the baby coming. It wouldn't be long. She needed to get to a hospital.

Somehow, she managed to get to the stairs without tripping. At some point, she gave up on stepping over the odd protrusions and simply ran. She stopped briefly to catch her breath but continued down the stairs as soon as possible.

She was halfway down when her foot caught the loose floorboard that she had noticed the day before. She scrambled for the railing to catch herself, but her fingertips barely grazed it and she went tumbling down the stairs. Her head cracked loudly as it hit the tile floor at the bottom.

She laid there on the cold floor, dazed and barely conscious. Blood pooled around her head, hot in the otherwise freezing house. She felt her body tense as the contractions began. The baby was coming, and she could do nothing about it. She couldn't even move. Her vision faded in and out, taking on a reddish hue as blood trickled into her eyes. She tried to whisper a prayer, but none came. The words of every prayer she had ever learned were lost to her now. There was only a silent hope to something greater. That hope went unheard.

With a final push, the baby slid from between Theresa's thighs and began its crying. It was at that moment that her vision faded for the last time, settling on an endless, icy darkness in which she drifted. The baby's crying continued for a while after that, though there was no one there to hear it. Only the freezing house which seemed to press down upon him, swaddling him in the fabric of a strange reality. Eventually, the crying stopped, and the baby became one with a different darkness, separate from its mother's, a blackness which belonged only to the shadows of the house.

THE CONFESSION

The congregation sat huddled in their pews, shoulder to shoulder, warm bodies jostling for position as they went about their worship. The choir sang hymns that echoed into the darkness which hung above them. Candles flickered weakly in their sconces and mad shadows danced across the marble floors. The people worshipped their god, whom they loved with all their hearts.

The priest stood in his pulpit, guiding them through this holiest of rituals. They spoke of the savior and they ate of his body. At times, they knelt in silent prayer, or they shouted jubilant cries of piety. They embraced one another and spoke of peace, love, and harmony. Eventually, the mass concluded, they stood in silence, and the priest gave his final blessing.

Before they could move from their seats, the priest spoke once more. "I will be taking confession today." A hushed silence fell upon the crowd. "Who among you would like to be forgiven?"

The congregation remained silent as they looked at one another, waiting for someone to speak up. It seemed an eternity passed in that silence. Tension filled the air, building and building, until it was finally broken when a young girl stepped forward from her pew.

She strode up the center aisle, and, as she did so, the church broke into a great chorus of cheers, claps, and whistles. This continued until she finally stood before the altar.

"Do you have sins to confess?" The priest asked as he stood before her.

"Yes, Father."

He gave her a warm and inviting smile. "All will be forgiven, my child." He gestured for her to stand behind the altar with him.

They stood in silence with bowed heads as a confessional booth was wheeled out onto the stage. The crowd remained hushed, watching carefully, smiles plastered on their faces. It had been many moons since the last confession. They worried that perhaps their god felt as if he'd been forgotten, his generosity ignored.

Finally, the stage was set. The priest and the woman sat down. They faced the crowd, a screen separating the two.

"What is your name?" The priest asked, his voice echoing off the cold stone of the church.

"Cassandra," the woman replied.

"And why are you here, Cassandra?"

"To confess my sins, Father."

"Are you a child of God?" He sounded almost accusatory.

"Yes."

"And yet you have sinned." A coldness permeated the priest's voice. Whispers sprang up amongst the congregation, but he held up his hand and they fell back into eager silence.

"I have made mistakes, Father. I'm afraid I have not

loved God enough." Tears shone in Cassandra's eyes and her voice trembled.

"Do you love him now?"

"I do."

"Then that is enough, child. What sin are you guilty of?"

"I have had impure thoughts. I have craved erotic and unclean acts." She stared at the floor and fiddled with her hands as she spoke.

"I knew it when I saw you. I could smell it on you." the priest's voice was thick with anger. "You are a disgusting creature, vulnerable to transgressions such as this."

Cassandra choked back a sob.

"I do not think I could ever love someone such as you. However, our God is much more forgiving. I hope you are thankful for his benevolence."

"I am," she said, tears rolling down her face.

At that moment a creaking sound filled the church. Members of the choir stood in the corner, slowly feeding rope to a pully as a black shape descended from the rafters. A dark cloth came into view. It hung about a dome-shaped structure. Sharp gasps came from the crowd as it slowly settled to the floor.

"Fornication of the mind is fornication nonetheless," the priest said. "Do you confess to this sin?"

"I do," Cassandra replied. Her voice took on a tone of cold acceptance.

"Then you shall be forgiven."

An altar boy walked forward and pulled away the black fabric to reveal a giant golden dome. An archway was cut into its front, and shadows moved within. The boy dashed away as the thing, their god, lumbered out the opening. It approached Cassandra, its limbs leaving trails of black ooze as they dragged across the floor. The woman sat in stony silence.

Finally, it stood mere inches from her then stopped, waiting. There was a moment of complete and utter silence, suspended in eternity, a final point of impending ecstasy.

"This is my body, I give unto you," Cassandra said.

It opened its gaping maw and began with her head. The crowd broke out into great shouts of joy and excited applause. They urged their god in its forgiveness. This continued until there was nothing left of Cassandra.

The thing lumbered back to its abode, its belly fat with sin, and was shrouded in cloth once more. The church remained silent as it was raised back into the darkness of the rafters where once again it listened from on high. When the cage was out of sight, the church echoed with one great utterance.

"Amen."

THE GROVE

Everything turned to darkness as we drove beneath the dense canopy of the Black Forest. I glanced over at Amanda in the passenger seat. She seemed entranced by the beauty of the trees. I didn't blame her. We'd been driving through the woods for days, but by then we'd reached the densest part of the forest. We hadn't seen any civilization for miles. We were completely alone, surrounded by trees that stood like dark giants in a fantastical world.

Amanda noticed me watching her and grinned before returning her gaze to the forest. My smile widened. Our honeymoon trip had been amazing so far. It was nice to just get out and explore. Both she and I had spent the past several years burdened by the workload of graduate school. But we were finally done, her with a master's degree in literature and me with a corresponding degree in philosophy.

"It makes a lot of sense," Amanda said suddenly from the passenger seat.

"What does?" I asked as I maneuvered the van around a large branch that had fallen into the road.

"All the local legends that eventually became the works of the Brothers Grimm. When you look at this dark landscape, you can't help but think there's something more out there."

I nodded. The forest truly was a strange place. It seemed as if it existed outside the normal bounds of our world, something on the fringes where anything might stumble through the swirls of fog and rows of looming trees. One felt very small in a place like this. Hell, everything felt small here, where something greater than our world seemed to weigh down upon the forest like a black sun.

I heard Amanda gasp in surprise beside me. My foot instinctively tapped the brakes, but I didn't come to a complete stop.

"What's wrong?"

She sighed and held her hands to her chest. "Nothing," she said, shaking her head. "I could have sworn I saw something giant walking through the forest." She laughed as she said it and rubbed her eyes. "I must be going crazy."

"Maybe you really did see something," I prodded. "If monsters did exist then this would be a perfect place for them to reside."

"Oh, shut up, Eric," she said, punching me in the shoulder.

I chuckled and continued driving. About twenty minutes later we came upon a clearing that seemed fit for camping. I parked off the side of the road and got out to examine the area. I was surprised to see that there were no signs of anyone having camped here before. The ground was completely untouched. We had taken a lot of strange, winding side roads, but I hadn't expected to get this far off the main path. I shrugged. The whole point of the trip was to get away from people, so I supposed this was ideal.

We took the bare necessities out of the van but decided to set things up later. Amanda wanted to relax and read for a while, so I chose to wander off and explore the forest. She sat curled up in the trunk of the van with a dense tome in her lap and waved as I left the clearing.

"Don't get lost!" She called.

"I won't!" I yelled back, waving in return.

As soon as I left the clearing I was assaulted on all sides by dense foliage and uneven terrain. I couldn't find any paths nearby. I was right about how far we'd gotten from the main path. No one had been here in ages. I paced with my hands thrust deep in my pockets, casually observing the beauty of the dark forest.

I noticed a strange number of large fallen branches on the ground. Normally, this would have been nothing worth noting, but they were all massive and seemed fresh. Many of the branches seemed to come from young, healthy trees. It didn't look as if they could have fallen in a storm. I shrugged it off and continued my walk.

After about thirty minutes, I decided to head back and begin setting up camp. I found Amanda curled up in the trunk, fast asleep. I considered leaving her there and just sleeping in the van rather than the tent, but the ground seemed soft and I wanted to stretch out in an open space. I gently woke her, and we began to set up camp.

It wasn't long before the tent was up, and we had a small fire burning. We sat around it, eating dinner in contented silence. Amanda rested her head on my shoulder as I finished my meal. By then the fire had burned low and I was feeling drowsy. We curled up in the tent and were soon fast asleep.

I woke to the sound of something moving through the forest. It sounded massive. Not bear massive, but even bigger, something gargantuan. I thought I heard one of those giant branches snap as whatever was out there stepped on it. I could hear it moving closer and closer to the clearing. I strained my ears and could have sworn I heard whispering. It was just barely audible, but it sounded as if dozens of voices were muttering to one another just out of earshot.

I struggled to keep my breathing under control. Amanda was still asleep beside me. She had always been an incredibly heavy sleeper. I considered waking her up but decided not to until I knew it was absolutely necessary.

Suddenly, there was a deafening crack followed by a crash and the sound of broken glass. The lumbering footsteps stomped around for a while then retreated back into the forest. I sat there for what seemed like an eternity, holding my breath until the forest returned to its typical nocturnal state.

The noise had woken Amanda and she asked what was going on, her voice groggy and confused. I grabbed my flashlight and stumbled out of the tent. My terror increased when I couldn't get the damn thing to turn on, but it finally flickered to life.

An enormous tree had fallen on the car. I whirled around, frantically looking for what had caused those footsteps. I turned my flashlight back to the tree and observed the damage. The van was almost certainly totaled. The tree had fallen in such a way that the engine was definitely crushed.

Amanda came out, still bleary-eyed, to see what was going on. She gasped when she saw the crushed van. "What happened?" She asked, putting her hands over her mouth.

I was still searching the depths of the forest for the thing I had heard. "Something pushed a tree on it," I said as I bounced my light from one spot to another, hoping it would happen upon the creature that did this.

"What?" Amanda asked.

"A fucking monster or something," I said. "I heard it walking around and then it pushed the tree down." My hands shook and it felt like I was breathing through a thin straw. No matter how hard I tried, I couldn't pull enough air into my lungs.

"Eric," Amanda said, putting her hands on my shoulders. "There's no monster. A tree just fell, that's all."

I couldn't control my breathing, and everything suddenly became too much. The sounds of crickets were too loud and the sensation of Amanda's hands on me felt wrong. It felt like I was suffocating.

"Hey," Amanda said softly. "You're having a panic attack again."

I was focused on fidgeting with my hands but nodded to show I had heard her. Everything was too stimulating, I simultaneously wanted to move and to lie down and feel nothing.

"Remember your breathing techniques." Amanda started to breathe loudly enough for me to hear. "Stay in sync with me."

I breathed with her and tried to relax. After a few minutes, I'd successfully calmed down. That was the first time I'd had a panic attack in years. They used to be constant. Any time I was under even the slightest amount of stress I would lose all control. My throat would feel like it was closing up and everything suddenly became too much to bear. I'd gotten better about it with time. I was a little ashamed that I had let myself lose control like that again, though I was thankful Amanda was there to help me.

"Are you okay?"

"I'm fine," I responded. "I guess I just got a little

freaked out." I was still sure I'd heard something outside the tent just before the tree fell, but I knew there was no point in arguing. If I had handled myself better, then perhaps I would have had some credibility. But having a panic attack right after claiming a monster destroyed our car didn't exactly help.

We ended up staying awake all night, hoping against all hope that once the sun arose our van might look salvageable. But, to no one's surprise, the morning sun only revealed more damage. The massive tree had fallen across the length of the vehicle, bisecting it and crushing it from end to end.

I examined the base of the tree. It hadn't snapped like an old or sick tree would. Rather, it had been uprooted, torn from the ground. I pointed it out to Amanda, and she said the soil must have been too loose for such a large tree. I doubted her appraisal but said nothing.

"What now?" Amanda asked.

I shrugged. "There's no cellphone service out here. We'll either have to find help or walk until we get somewhere with service."

"One of us should stay here with the stuff. Someone might come by on the road."

I thought back to the thing I'd heard the night before and shook my head. "I think we should stick together. If someone driving by sees the crushed van, they'll probably call in a search party anyway. We can leave a note saying we went looking for help."

Amanda nodded her agreement and we began to pack. We decided to bring only the bare necessities, as we might have to walk for a long time. I recalled that we hadn't seen any signs of civilization for many miles while driving here, so we decided to follow the road in the opposite direction in the hopes that we would come across another town.

We packed as much food as we could carry in addition to sleeping bags, the tent, and other miscellaneous supplies. With more than a few spare glances back at the wreckage of our van, we set off in search of help.

We walked along the road for several hours. I began to notice more large branches blocking the path as well as countless fallen trees. I realized that if anyone lived nearby, they would have already cleared the road, but hope kept us moving forward. The last town we'd passed was too far behind us to reasonably walk there.

Eventually, the sun dipped low in the sky and our legs began to tire. I observed that the road seemed even worse than before. The sensation that we were moving further from civilization sat like a cold block of ice in my gut. Amanda didn't seem to be as affected. She was just as observant as me and had surely noticed the road's condition, but she had always been more inclined toward optimistic thought. She probably still believed that we would stumble upon some village tucked away between the hills.

We moved to the side of the road at the next clearing we passed and began to set up camp. The sun hung just above the horizon as I struggled to assemble the tent. One of the pieces had snapped when we took it down earlier, and I had to improvise. As I was doing so, I heard a noise in the forest to my left.

It sounded like a large creature running through the underbrush. The thing sounded huge. My heart began to pound as it drew closer. I couldn't help but recall the creature I had heard the night before. I grabbed one of the tent's plastic rods and wielded like a weapon. The thing bounded closer and closer until a large deer sprang from the shrubbery and ran past. It nearly barreled over Amanda as it disappeared into the forest on the other side of the clearing.

"Holy shit," I said. My voice was shaky.

Amanda laughed nervously. "Were you planning on killing it with that?" she said, gesturing to the thin, flexible rod I held.

"Better than nothing." I shrugged and returned to assembling the tent.

Eventually, I managed to get it together and began to help Amanda build a fire. We tried to make it as big as possible in hopes the smoke would alert people to our location. We sat around the roaring blaze until the moon was high above us, our hopes dying with every passing moment. After a couple of hours, we decided to douse the flames.

We were both exhausted and Amanda fell asleep almost as soon as she laid down. However, I tossed and turned for much of the night. I couldn't tear my thoughts away from that enormous thing I'd heard the night before or the strange whispering that accompanied it. However, I managed to drift into a fitful sleep after several hours.

Suddenly Amanda was rousing me, and a high-pitched sound filled the air. She urged me to get up over and over, her voice frantic. It was still dark outside. I rubbed the sleep from my eyes and sat up only to realize that the high-pitched screaming was the sound of a baby crying in the forest.

"Do you hear that?" Amanda said.

I nodded. The sound was unmistakable. A baby was crying somewhere out there in the darkness. We both moved at the same time to grab our flashlights and stood outside listening intently. The noise came from the forest to our right.

Amanda started in that direction, but I grabbed her arm and held her back.

"What are you doing?" She hissed.

"What if it's a trap?"

"A trap? Are you insane? There's a fucking baby out there that might need our help and you think it's a *trap*?" She jerked her arm away and glared at me.

"Look, it's just that something isn't right here and I-"

She began running toward the source of the sound before I had a chance to finish. I chased after her as the beam of my flashlight bounced around haphazardly. We entered the dense underbrush, and for a moment I thought I'd lost her. But I caught a glimpse of her red shirt in a tangle of trees and veered in that direction. The baby's cries grew louder as approached.

I burst through a wall of shrubbery to find Amanda standing before a massive twisted tree. She looked up at it in a daze. The crying sounds came from where she stood, and I briefly thought she held the baby in her arms. But then I saw the terrible truth.

A child's face pressed out of the tree's wood, its expression contorted in agony and its mouth thrown open in a scream of torment. The face strained at the wooden prison that entrapped it as if trying to tear itself free. The wood flexed around it like rubber. Both Amanda and I stood frozen before the monstrous sight. What the fuck was going on?

Before I could say anything, a great wooden limb swooped down and impaled Amanda. It snatched her limp form from the earth, and she disappeared in the tangled darkness of the canopy. I watched it all happen as if it were in slow motion. My breath caught in my throat, and I felt something between a scream and a sob begin to rise in my chest.

Before I could react, a countless number of faces sprouted from the wood of the tree. They all sighed and writhed in a tumultuous expression of ecstasy. Their tongues reached out from the wood and I watched as thick red fluid ran down the bark. The whole tree seemed to shiver with pleasure as the blood entered its eager, waiting mouths. The faces, now satisfied, silently retreated back into the monstrous tree.

I stood there in stunned silence, frozen by a horrible concoction of terror, panic, grief, and confusion. The spell broke when a horrible creaking, tearing sound filled the air. The trunk of the tree before me split in half. One of the halves raised itself, its roots only loosely connected to the ground, and stepped toward me. Holy fuck, the thing was walking.

I stared in awe for a moment, but then it took another lumbering step and I was struck with terror. I immediately turned and ran in the other direction. As if reacting to my movement, the tree sped up and its tendrilled legs began a steady march behind me. Whispers filled the air, and I spared a glance over my shoulder to see that innumerable faces had once again sprouted from the tree's bark.

I nearly tripped and turned back to watch my footing. One wrong move and it would be over. That thing would get me, and I would meet the same fate as Amanda. That thought almost stopped me dead in my tracks. Amanda was dead. My wife was dead. What point was there anymore? But something kept me running. Despite my grief, I still had a sense of self-preservation, and nothing terrified me more than the thought of those twisted limbs carrying me into the darkness.

Branches crashed down around me as the sprawling limbs of the creature tore through the tops of other trees. Nothing seemed to slow it down and it maintained a steady pace as it hunted me. Suddenly a voice rang out from behind.

"Eric," the voice said. It was soothing and completely at odds with the current situation. I turned to see a lone face peering down at me. It was Amanda's. Her features were largely obscured by the tree's bark, but I knew it was her. A gentle smile spread across her face.

I slowed down at the sight of my wife, but the looming presence of the tree from which she protruded brought me back to reality. I faced forward and tried to ignore her cries behind me.

I veered into a dense thicket of trees, which seemed to momentarily slow the enormous creature. Deafening cracks filled the air as it tore through the forest. Briefly out of sight, I dove behind a wide oak and shrouded myself in foliage.

Now free, the thing slowed and began to look for me. Nothing about its movement was quiet, and I heard it circling me, growing ever closer.

"Eriiiic," The thing said in Amanda's voice. "Come on out, honey. It's okay. We like it here, and you will too."

I tried to control my breathing, but it became difficult. I could feel another panic attack rising. My breath came in short spurts and it felt like the underbrush was suffocating me. It took every ounce of my willpower to not burst out into the open air. I remembered the breathing techniques I had always done with Amanda and tried to focus. A few moments later I was under control, though only barely, and listening intently for the creature. I hadn't heard it move in a while.

I heard a whipping sound and a great branch swooped down and tore at the foliage above me. It just barely missed me, shredding the plants that had previously concealed my form. I was completely out in the open.

I dashed forward, just barely dodging another limb. The thing came crashing through the underbrush, wildly swinging for me, each time missing me by mere inches.

"Eric, please." I heard my wife's voice behind me. "I just want to hold you in my arms. Don't you love me?"

It pained me to ignore her, but I knew Amanda was gone. That voice belonged to the tree, and I wouldn't fall for its tricks. I ran on endlessly until it felt like I would collapse at any moment. I could feel the ground shaking beneath my feet as the thing pounded after me. It was tireless, never stopping or slowing. I knew it would catch me eventually.

Just then I saw that the forest thinned out ahead. I thought I had come across another clearing when I burst forth into the open air. I stood in a massive field that led up a steep hill. The forest was behind me and I saw nothing but plains stretching endlessly ahead.

I glanced back to see the towering tree-like creature standing motionless at the edge of the forest. It had stopped and only watched as I ran across the grass. Perhaps it couldn't leave. It made sense. After all, the forest was its domain. Maybe that's why no one had ever reported seeing them. They only exist in a limited and unexplored area.

Regardless of why, I had won. I began laughing maniacally and threw my hands up in victory. The terrible events of the past forty-eight hours still weighed heavily upon me, but for the moment I was triumphant, and I relished it. I kept running, my veins still pumping with adrenaline.

As I climbed the hill before me, a great chorus filled the air. The voices of hundreds of people rose from the other side. It sounded like some kind of festival or something. I realized that there must be a village nearby. That must have been why the tree stopped chasing me. It was avoiding civilization. A sense of relief filled me, and I eagerly crested the hill.

I looked down to see hundreds of those trees, each one riddled with faces that chattered and whispered and writhed amongst themselves. I froze at the grotesque sight. Suddenly the voices stopped, and the thousands of faces turned towards me in silence. Then, with bellows of ecstasy and excitement, they tore their roots from the earth and began to hunt.

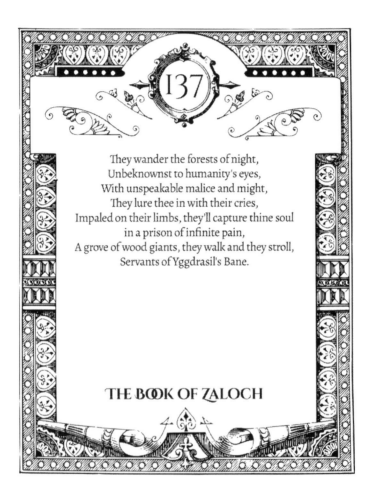

137

They wander the forests of night,
Unbeknownst to humanity's eyes,
With unspeakable malice and might,
They lure thee in with their cries,
Impaled on their limbs, they'll capture thine soul
in a prison of infinite pain,
A grove of wood giants, they walk and they stroll,
Servants of Yggdrasil's Bane.

THE BOOK OF ZALOCH

THE MIMIC

The worst day of my life started as a casual summer evening. My friend Michael and I loaded up the trunk of his car. His dingy gray Toyota was laden with backpacks, food, a tent, and all the makings of a camping trip.

However, this trip carried with it a certain finality. In a way, it was a goodbye, a passage from one stage of life to another. We were nearing the end of summer, and our freshman year of college was about to start. I had decided to attend a local community college, while Michael found himself enrolled at a technical institute a few states over. Separated by an eight-hour drive, we would be farther apart than ever before.

I stared at the bumper of the car, lost in thought. Michael and I had known each other ever since we could remember. Our mothers had been friends and introduced us as playmates when we were babies. And now we were adults, headed our separate ways. I knew it wasn't as tragic as it seemed. We would still see each other during breaks, and it's not as if we couldn't stay in touch during the semester or visit one another occasionally. Nonetheless, it felt like the end of something I could never get back, a farewell to our younger selves and the friendship we had fostered.

"Stephen!"

Michael's shout jerked me from my thoughts. He leaned against the driver's side door and tapped his watch. "We have to get going. I want to make sure we have enough daylight to explore."

I nodded and moved to get in the car. Michael had always been an outdoorsman and took any opportunity to spend his time in some far-flung forest. I preferred to stay inside, but usually tagged along because I enjoyed his company. This had been our dynamic for years now as he excitedly dragged me along to every distant, unpopulated area he could find.

However, this trip was a little different. When Michael initially suggested it, I refused immediately. But, as our time together drew to an end and he kept nagging, I finally relented. Our destination was the Golgotha Caves, a cave system about two hours north in an isolated area between our town and the next.

I sat in the passenger seat and fastened my seatbelt. I glanced at Michael. "Are you sure about this?"

He smiled, a hint of mischief in his eyes as always. "Of course! We've been planning this for months. We can't back out now."

I sighed and leaned my head back against the headrest. The Golgotha Caves were incredibly dangerous, and the local government had forbidden anyone from exploring them for the past fifty years. Countless people had become lost and died there, and the area was prone to landslides and cave-ins. Not to mention the plethora of horror stories about that place. Ghost sightings, strange sounds, mysterious lights. The Golgotha Caves had it all.

Michael started the engine and turned the radio up.

Music blared from our open windows as he pulled out of the driveway and veered north. I know now that I never should have agreed to go to those cursed caves. It may have seemed worth it at the time, but nothing could ever make up for the terrible things that happened there.

We reached the caves about three hours later. Some traffic on the interstate had made our trip a little longer than intended. We were forced to park several miles away from the caves since any roads that led near them had been shut down long ago Supposedly, security patrols were stationed around the area to catch anyone who tried driving off-road.

Our plan was to hike a circuitous route, remaining careful to avoid other people along the way. The hike was long, and our heavy gear made it even longer, but the terrain was surprisingly flat and easy to navigate. We found the caves after only a couple of hours.

Michael and I had agreed that we would hide our gear and enter the caves as soon as we found them. That way, we were guaranteed at least a little time to explore if we got caught. Additionally, our camp might alert people to our presence, and we decided it was best to set up around dusk.

We stashed our gear in some shrubbery near a cove of unnaturally tall trees figuring they would be easy to find later in the evening. With everything safely hidden, we headed off to find the main entrance to the caves.

It took a little searching, but we eventually found it. Though it was early afternoon and everything was bathed in the golden glow of the sun, the enormous cavern before us managed to look menacing nonetheless. Great stalactites hung down from the ceiling and stalagmites rose from the floor, making it seem like the mouth of some giant creature just waiting to swallow us whole. A cold and thoughtless beast that devoured all who dared to near it.

Michael clapped me on the back. "Let's go, Stephen!" He began to walk toward the cave with me reluctantly trailing behind. Several signs scattered about warned us against trespassing and alerted us to the dangers of cave-ins. We ignored them and walked right in.

Despite my initial impression, the caves seemed normal once you got inside. They were just like any other. Dark, wet tunnels of gray stone. They presented their own dangers: sharp rocks, steep drop-offs, and potential cave-ins. But there was nothing supernatural about it. The caves were almost eerie in their normality. One would think a location that inspired so many folktales and ghost stories would be more interesting.

Michael and I explored for the better part of an hour, chatting and bantering the whole time. Our voices echoed strangely in the craggy depths, causing a shiver to run down my spine. For hours we wandered about, leaving a trail of string behind us so we could find our way back.

Eventually, I became tired. While I hadn't been looking forward to a dangerous trip, I had hoped it would be more entertaining than this. There was nothing but the endless gray walls of stone and rocks that threatened to trip us with every step. I kept urging Michael to turn around so we could relax outside, and he eventually began to wear down too.

We were just about to turn back when Michael noticed a narrow tunnel to our right. It was barely visible, just a crack in the wall. It was only by sheer luck that he managed to spot it. And what foul luck it was. If I could go back in time, I would have urged him to forget he ever saw that tunnel. I would have dragged him out of the cave by force if I had to. But I did none of those things. And that is something that I must live with.

Without saying a word, Michael gravitated toward the tunnel. I sighed and followed him. He had that look in his eye again. He was going to explore that niche and nothing I said would stop him. I stood behind him as he beamed his flashlight down the narrow passage. It didn't get any wider, but it didn't seem to get any narrower either.

"I bet this leads somewhere cool," Michael said.

"I bet it's a hundred yards of squirming then a dead end."

Michael smirked. "Well if that's the case then we're only adding a couple hundred more yards to our trip."

Damn. He had me there. I was already cold and tired, but I decided to oblige once more and followed suit as he turned sideways and edged his way through the narrow crevice. It wasn't too narrow, and we had no trouble making progress so long as we were angled sideways.

The passage turned out to be much longer than a hundred yards. It seemed to stretch on in an endless straight line, the esophagus of some cataclysmic beast, closing in around us with suffocating rigor.

Every time I grumbled about wanting to turn back, Michael would reassure me that we were certainly on the cusp of some awesome cavern or beautiful underground lake.

Just as I was about to insist on turning back, I heard Michael gasp ahead of me.

"Steve, come here!" he shouted.

Thinking he was injured, I rushed forward and nearly fell in the process. He had gotten farther ahead of me than I initially thought. I frantically aimed my flashlight down the dark, ragged corridor in an attempt to see what had happened.

I had just noticed a change in the way my light hit the walls when I stumbled out of the narrow tunnel and into a large cavern. Michael stood in front of me gazing around in amazement.

"Jesus man, you scared me," I said, trying to catch my breath. Michael neglected to respond. He continued to stare around the cavern with slack-jawed wonder.

"Michael!" I snapped my fingers to get his attention. He still ignored me. I reached out to grab his shoulder. "It's just a cav-" My words were cut short as I finally processed my surroundings.

We weren't in a normal cavern. The walls were perfectly smooth, unmarred by any cracks or rock formations. They even seemed to be polished, as they reflected the glow of our flashlights. We were standing in what could only be described as a room. It was perfectly circular, and every inch of it shone reflectively. It couldn't have been natural. There was a consciousness to it, a distinctly human intent in its construction. Someone must have carved this area out and sanded it until everything was perfectly smooth.

"This is incredible." I had barely whispered the words, but they sounded like a shout in the cold silence of that room. Michael didn't respond. He had grown very still all of a sudden. Without warning, he marched forward. There was intense purpose and curiosity in his posture.

As he moved, I saw what had caught his attention. There was a door in the wall directly across from us. Or, it seemed like a door. Unlike most doorways, this wasn't rectangular. It was a perfect square. A person could climb through it if they wanted to, but it seemed less like an entrance and more like a window for observation.

A thick metal door blocked the opening. It was plain except for a strange symbol carved into its center. The carving was unlike anything I had ever seen - a strange mixture of hard angles and perfect circles all closing in on one another. Looking at it made my head hurt.

Michael made his way to the door and I followed close behind. He stopped just short of it and we both stood in silence for a moment.

"I don't know if we should open it," I said, my voice echoing strangely in the chamber. "What if there's some kind of toxic chemical on the other side or dangerous wiring?"

Michael shook his head. "There hasn't been any industrial work here for over a century. The passages are too narrow, and the caves are unstable."

I was about to respond when, without warning, he grabbed the door by the handle and jerked it open. The hinges screeched a terrible, jarring chorus and the door swung wide. There was nothing but darkness beyond.

Michael shined his light through the opening. It seemed to be another chamber resembling the one we were in. He swept his light back and forth in wide arcs. On his second pass, we both caught a glimpse of something white. Michael immediately stopped and focused his beam on the shape.

A sudden sinking feeling came over me and my blood ran cold. A woman was laying on the ground with a chain that led from her ankle to a fixture on the wall. As soon as Michael's flashlight fell on her, she glanced up. I jumped at her sudden movement.

"Holy shit," Michael whispered. I stepped forward to observe more closely. The woman had tan skin and dark flowing hair. There was something Native American in her appearance. She wore a white dress covered in dirt and her skin was crossed with thin, pale scars.

The situation seemed immediately apparent. Some sick person had been keeping this woman locked down in the caves for their own entertainment. I shuddered to think of what had been done to her. All alone in the belly of this stony beast, subjected to unspeakable horrors.

The woman opened her mouth and wailed at us. There were no words. Just a cry of pain and suffering. I was about to climb through the door to help her when Michael leapt into action. He threw one leg over the doorway's ledge and looked to me.

"Focus your flashlight on her so I know where I'm going," he said. I nodded and trained my flashlight on the chained woman.

Michael swung his other leg over the opening and began to quickly stride toward her. I saw the small circle of his light gliding across the floor as he walked. I turned my eyes back to the woman. She continued her wordless plea for help, and I watched as she reached out towards Michael's approaching form.

She started to say something, but the words weren't English. They didn't even seem to be words at all. Her mouth darted through consonants and vowels in a way no human's ever could. My skin crawled as I listened to the crude mockery of language. I told myself she was simply in shock and saying nonsense, but something about the way she spoke felt so wrong. She began to quiet down as Michael got closer. His light was only a few feet away from her.

Just as he was about to reach her, the woman turned to face me. She shouldn't have been able to see me past my flashlight, but I felt her eyes lock with mine. I expected to see fear or even hope in her eyes, but there was nothing behind them. They were completely blank. Everyone's eyes go blank from time to time when they're distracted or daydreaming, but this was different. There truly was nothing behind them. It felt as if I was staring into a cold, vast emptiness contained within some pale imitation of a human body.

"Michael!" I shouted, but it was too late. He had already reached the woman. With a quick, snakelike motion she grabbed his ankle. I heard him shout in surprise then go completely silent. My breath caught in my throat as I kept my flashlight trained on the pair.

Michael had gone still, but now he began to shake uncontrollably. It wasn't like a shiver. He was vibrating, and a strange hum filled the air. It was as if a swarm of angry hornets was inside of him fighting to break free. Without warning, he went limp. His posture lost all semblance of consciousness. In that moment something told me there was nothing left of Michael.

The thing that was Michael turned toward me. A slow, eerie turn that was completely at odds with the current situation.

"Come here, Stephen." His voice was completely flat, without a hint of emotion. "I think I'm going to need some help with this chain. You wouldn't want to leave your mother out in the cold, would you?"

I glanced back at the woman and my breath caught in my throat. She had changed. She was no longer the dark-haired girl she had been. Instead, my mother laid there bound in chains. I almost ran to her. I almost leapt through the doorway and tried to save her from this cruel fate. But there was something wrong about the situation.

I blinked and shook my head. My mother had died

years ago. I remembered going to her funeral, hugging all the visitors as they told me how sorry they were, and later standing over her grave with tears in my eyes. That *thing* in there wasn't my mother any more than the other one was my friend Michael.

I'd like to say that I did something heroic. That I tried to save Michael or at the very least barricaded the door so that those creatures could never break free. But I did neither of those things. I simply ran.

As soon as I bolted for the door, the creature let go of Michael. I watched over my shoulder as he fell limply to the floor. He had become nothing more than a puppet. I felt a sob rise in my throat. But I didn't turn back.

I ran and ran and ran. It's a miracle I found my way out of those caves. I had completely forgotten about the trail of string we had left. I blindly ran through the twisting passages, convinced those things were right behind me, until I was suddenly free of the stone prison and running through the forest.

-

So now I sit here, writing all of this down for whoever might someday stumble upon it. My memories of that cave, of that thing, have plagued me ever since. And now it's loose, all because of me. I fear what chaos it will wreak upon the world. If anyone finds this, know that this is both an admission of my guilt and an apology. I'm so sorry.

I've never told any of this to anyone. But I'm satisfied with the knowledge that it lies here for all who might look upon it. Hate me for what I did or forgive me for it. It matters not.

I must be going now. Mother is starting to become irritated. She's been outside shouting my name all night. It sounds like she might be hurt. I don't have the heart to ignore her any longer.

THE DARK WEB

Henry was a shy and reclusive boy of eleven. While most children his age enjoyed playing outside and spending time with their friends, Henry preferred to remain indoors and play video games. They were his sole pastime, and he spent every waking moment playing them over his winter break. He had recently gotten a new console for Christmas, a Nintendo Switch, and could reliably be found in his bedroom engrossed in some game. While his parents were rather lenient compared to most, they also knew that this behavior was unhealthy for Henry. He needed to socialize and spend time away from electronics. Because of this, Henry's mother decided to take away his Nintendo Switch and hide it.

Upon realizing his favorite device was gone, Henry was furious. The young boy stomped over to his mother and demanded she tell him where it is.

"No," she said sternly. "You need to do something else today. Go outside or read a book. I don't care. But no video games."

Henry whined as children often do, but his mother remained resolute. Undeterred, he went to his father and asked for his game back. However, his father also said no in a way that left no room for negotiation. Henry stormed out of his father's office and began to wander the house looking for something, anything, to do. But nothing could keep his attention. He had planned on spending all day playing his Switch, and now it seemed there was nothing left.

He finally settled on wasting time on the computer in his room. His parents had neglected to take that, and it would have been a major hassle to transport anyway. However, nothing on the internet interested him. He only wanted to play on his Nintendo Switch. He was fixated on it and nothing else mattered. There were a million things he *could* do, but only one thing he *wanted* to do. He fumed at the unfairness of his parents.

Henry looked up to see that he was on a strange website. He had no memory of how he had gotten there but thought he had stumbled onto an odd corner of the internet by accident. The website consisted of a still image of a laughing jester surrounded by a red light. It took up almost the entirety of the screen except for a white box at the bottom of the display.

He moved to exit the website when his computer dinged and a message appeared in the white box. *That's strange*, he thought. He could have sworn he had turned the computer's sound off.

"Hello," the message in the chatbox read.

Henry stared at it for a moment. There didn't seem to be a place for him to respond. "Who are you?" He said more to himself than anything.

"My name is Zyrdectus. Zyrdectus the clown," said another chat. It was as if the computer had heard him.

"You can hear me?" Henry asked, incredulous.

"Of course," Zyrdectus responded. "I can see you

too."

"How?"

"I see all," he responded simply.

"My name's Henry," the boy responded.

"I know," the next message read. The image of the jester was strange. There seemed to be dark tendrils hanging from its colorful outfit. He peered closer. They weren't easy to make out, but the strange tendrils almost looked like strings. It was as if the jester was a puppet.

"How do you know that?" He asked.

"I know all."

Henry sat in thoughtful silence for a moment. "If you know everything, then where did my mom hide my game?"

"I'll tell you if you do something for me first," Zyrdectus replied. Henry squinted at the screen. It almost looked as if the clown figure had moved closer. Was it actually a video? He squinted but there was no doubt that it was a still image.

"What's that?" Henry asked.

"I need you to promise to be my friend. That's what friends do, after all. They help each other. I can't help you unless you're my friend.

Henry hesitated. He knew making friends was always good, but still, he had that uneasy butterfly feeling in his stomach that grown-ups warned him about. He felt like he was about to do something wrong. But then he thought about how much he wanted his game back. He decided to look on the bright side of things. He had never really had a friend before. It felt nice that someone wanted to be friends with him.

"Okay," Henry said. "I'll be your friend."

The screen flickered black and, for a split second,

Henry thought he saw something in its darkness, a deeper shade of black that writhed on the lifeless display. But, in less than a second, it was gone, replaced by the same still image that had been there all along.

"It is done," a message displayed on the screen. "Your game is hidden in the top drawer of your mother's dresser wrapped in an old blue sweater."

Henry could hear his mother watching TV in the living room, so he shot up and went directly to his parents' bedroom. He was doubtful of what the dark figure had told him but decided to look anyway. He opened the dresser's top drawer and peered inside. A blue sweater sat atop the other clothes.

Henry pulled it out and felt that it was heavier than it should have been. He unfolded it to find his Nintendo Switch inside. His face broke into a wide grin. It seemed that Zyrdectus had been right. He really did know everything. Henry accepted the clown's omniscience with the same unquestioning faith with which children accept all things.

He returned to the computer where the screen had gone dark. The strange website was gone. Henry tried to find it again, but he had no memory of having gotten there in the first place and it didn't appear in his search history. He was disappointed that his friend was gone, but at least he still had his game back. He spent the rest of the day playing it and almost forgot about the eerie jester that had appeared on his computer.

The next day his mother stormed into his room, furious that he had found and stolen back his game. She jerked it from his hands and swore to hide it better this time. Thus, Henry went about the same ritual as the day before. He wandered around, looking for anything to keep his at-

95

tention. But there was nothing. He couldn't tear his mind from the game. He had been fixated it for weeks now, and he had only become even more obsessed with it since meeting Zyrdectus. He wondered if he could find that website again so the clown could tell him where the game was hidden now.

He moved to his computer and was surprised to find that the site was already up. That still image was there again. The jester seemed closer this time, its jubilant outfit taking up more of the screen now. Henry saw a darkness behind the laughing figure. There appeared to be a shadow which seemed to envelop the clown before it. He thought it was strange but ignored it.

"Hello," he said. He tried to say the clown's name, but it was long and difficult to pronounce. "How did you get on my computer?"

"I'm always here when you need me," it responded.

"Do you know where my game is?"

"Yes."

"Where is it?" Henry asked.

There was no response for a moment and the cursor on the screen blinked for what seemed like an eternity. Finally, a response appeared. "It's locked in the trunk of your father's car. He has the keys with him."

Henry considered the message for a moment. "How am I supposed to get it then?"

"There is a way."

"How?" Henry asked.

"I'm going to tell you some things," Zyrdectus responded. "Repeat them to your father exactly as I say them."

Henry nodded and focused intently on the next messages he received. He had a vague inkling of what they said, but they were confusing. Nonetheless, he nodded after having read them all and went to his father.

"Hey bud," Henry's father said as he entered the room.

Henry walked up to him and stood silently for a moment. For some reason, his father felt a sense of impending doom. He glanced at his son and nearly flinched. A dark figure stood behind the boy. Henry's father blinked and the strange sight was gone. He shook his head and stared at the space where it had been. The figure had looked like a man with strings that hung down to Henry's limbs. For the briefest of moments, it had looked like someone controlling a puppet. A chill ran down his spine. It must have been his imagination.

"I want my game back," Henry said.

His father sighed. "You know I can't give it back. Surely you can go a single day without it? It's not healthy for you to play video games all the time."

"If you don't give it back, I'm going to tell mom."

Henry's father looked confused. "Mom already knows. She's the one who took it from you in the first place."

Henry shook his head. "Not about that. I'm going to tell her about Hannah."

His father kept a straight face, but he suddenly became very pale. "Who's Hannah?"

"The girl whose pussy you've been fucking. The one you meet in the dirty little motels where everyone knows what you're doing with that filthy whore."

His father seemed angry at first, but as Henry continued, his face became a mask of terror. At that moment, the little boy before him seemed much more than a child.

"How did you..." He trailed off.

"Give my game back and I won't tell mom."

Henry's father seemed dumbfounded for a moment, but he gathered himself and spoke calmly. "Okay bud, I'll go get it." He knelt down so he could look Henry in the eyes. "But you have to promise not to tell mommy."

Henry nodded. His father left and returned a few moments later with the Nintendo Switch. His hands trembled as he handed it to his son. "Here you go. Remember what you promised."

"I won't tell her."

His father gave him a relieved smile, patted him on the shoulder, and left the room. Henry returned to his computer where he found that the website was, once again, gone. He shrugged it off and went on to play his game.

Eventually, Henry's mother realized that he had his game once again. His father claimed that Henry had spent enough time away from it and deserved to have it back. This led to an argument that lasted well into the night. Henry paid it no mind, as he was absorbed in his video games.

Henry didn't visit the strange website or talk to Zyrdectus for a long time after that. His mother took his game several times, but the website never appeared for him. The jester had abandoned him. Henry was angry at him for that. The clown was supposed to be his friend. Friends didn't abandon each other. It felt as if he had been forgotten.

One day, several months later, Henry's father gently asked him to come into the living room so they could talk. His mother was sitting on the couch, her eyes red from crying. They sat in silence for a moment then told him that they were getting divorced. They explained his father had done some bad things, and they couldn't be together anymore.

Henry wasn't particularly distraught by this new information. He didn't care if his parents stayed together, nor did he see how this affected him. He had never really cared if his parents loved each other. However, what his parents said next upset him. They told him that they would be moving houses. His mom and dad would be living separately, and neither could afford to keep the house they currently lived in.

Henry cried at that. He loved his house. There was plenty of space, and his bedroom was large. He had never lived anywhere else. This home held the entirety of his life's experiences and leaving that behind felt like losing a dear friend.

His parents tried to comfort him, but he ran off to be alone. He sat in his room and sobbed. Where would he keep his things? He didn't want to live in two different houses. He wanted to stay exactly where he was. He was happy here.

It wasn't until late that night that he stopped crying. He was worn out and began getting ready for bed. He slipped into his pajamas and brushed his teeth. He could hear his parents snoring in the room across from his. Normally they would have scolded him for staying up so late, but he figured they were being lenient after seeing how upset he was.

As Henry moved to get into bed, he noticed that his computer had turned on. That strange website was on the screen once again. It had been months since he'd last seen it, and it took him a moment to recognize the laughing figure. He moved to the computer and sat down.

"Are you here to help me?" He whispered, careful that his parents didn't hear him.

"Yes," Zyrdectus responded.

"My parents say we have to move."

"I know," the jester said.

"How do I stop it?"

"I'm going to give you some instructions. You must follow them exactly as I say and don't ask any questions. If you do this, then you can stay here forever."

"Okay," Henry said. Zyrdectus had helped him before, and he trusted the clown to help him now.

Zyrdectus gave him a series of instructions and told him to return to the computer once he was done. Henry read the directions intently and nodded as he did so. He didn't see how they would help his situation, but he decided to do what the jester said. Who was Henry to argue with someone who knew everything?

He snuck into his parents' bedroom and looked where Zyrdectus had directed him. He had to move quietly, but he managed to find it behind the dresser: a small white box plugged into the wall. Henry unplugged it as he had been instructed and watched as the box's blue light went out. He returned to the computer, box in hand, and was given further instructions. The things he was told to do seemed strange, even dangerous in a vague way that Henry didn't really understand, but he paid close attention to what Zyrdectus said and agreed to do it.

He went into the basement and found the big, white water heater. As he had been instructed, he circled around to the backside where a large silver tube connected it to the wall. It was higher than Henry had anticipated, and he had to stand on a chair in order to reach it. The pipe seemed sturdy and he wasn't sure if he could do what Zyrdectus asked. After mulling over the problem for a moment, he came up with an idea.

Henry grasped the pipe and jumped from the chair, bringing all of his weight down upon it. It didn't break, but it wobbled considerably. He dropped to the floor and climbed back up to do it again. This time it worked, and he heard a sharp hissing sound as the pipe snapped at one of its junctions.

Henry moved to the furnace next and repeated the same process. This time the pipe was sturdier, and it took several more tries. However, he eventually succeeded and heard another sharp hiss as it broke.

Zyrdectus had told him to return after breaking the pipes and await further instruction. He came back to the computer and sat, waiting for the strange man to say something.

"Hello," Henry called to his screen. There was no response. He sat there for two more hours, waiting for some kind of message. None came, and he suddenly began to feel very groggy. His stomach turned and he felt vomit rising in his throat. Just barely making it to the bathroom, he kneeled in front of the toilet and retched.

When he stopped vomiting, he found that breathing seemed difficult and his vision was blurry. He thought that he had somehow gotten sick and decided to lie down. Zyrdectus could wait. His head was aching, and he still felt nauseous. Henry closed his eyes and drifted off to a place beyond sleep where darkness was eternal and Zyrdectus waited for him with open arms.

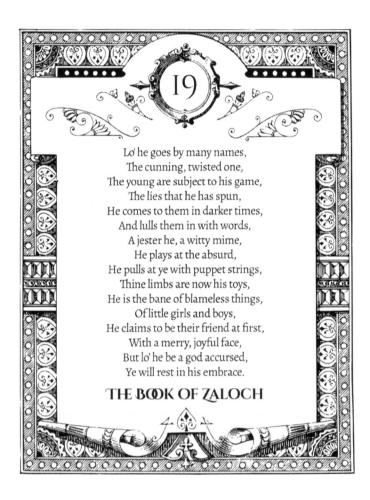

19

Lo' he goes by many names,
The cunning, twisted one,
The young are subject to his game,
The lies that he has spun,
He comes to them in darker times,
And lulls them in with words,
A jester he, a witty mime,
He plays at the absurd,
He pulls at ye with puppet strings,
Thine limbs are now his toys,
He is the bane of blameless things,
Of little girls and boys,
He claims to be their friend at first,
With a merry, joyful face,
But lo' he be a god accursed,
Ye will rest in his embrace.

THE BOOK OF ZALOCH

GHOST TOWN

The town appeared out of nowhere. I glanced away from the road for a moment, and when I turned back it was there, looming on the horizon, stark against the setting sun. For all I knew, it could have snapped into existence at that very moment. Or, perhaps it was there all along and I had overlooked it. I wish it had remained overlooked. I wish I had just kept driving and never glanced back at that monstrous place. But no amount of wishing can change the things that happened there.

"Well, would you look at that," I said as I saw the town on the horizon. The Black Rock Desert was completely flat for miles around, so the town was easily visible despite being quite far away. It grew closer with every step. Even then I thought it looked strange, like a great predator that sat waiting for prey to enter its domain.

"What?" Elton said from the passenger seat. He held a giant map in front of him, obscuring his view through the windshield.

"We're coming up on a town."

Elton lowered the map and peered through the window, narrowing his eyes at the approaching silhouette. Without saying anything he began to once again scrutinize the map.

"There shouldn't be anything for miles," he said a moment later.

"Don't look a gift horse in the mouth," I said. "I don't think this thing's going to work much longer." I grimaced as the car made yet another horrid grinding sound. It shuddered and, for a moment, I thought we would have to stop. But the shuddering ceased, and our poor Subaru kept trudging along.

"I suppose you're right," Elton said before returning to his map.

The trip had been a disaster from the start. It was supposed to be a way for us to get away from things and enjoy ourselves, but it had been anything but enjoyable. The plan had been simple: start in Texas, drive to California, then make our way up the West Coast until we got to Seattle. We were supposed to stop at various locales on the way, including Las Vegas. But that's not the way things had gone.

Every time I proposed a place to stop, a sight to see, or even a restaurant to try, Elton would turn it down in his usual terse manner. It was frustrating, although I can't say I blamed him. The trip was mostly for him. His fiancé Gwen had gone missing several months ago, and he had been a different person ever since. He was always grim, dull-eyed, seeming to observe everything before him with the same lethargy with which a tired student watches a boring lecture.

The circumstances of her disappearance were haunting. She was supposed to meet him for their wedding rehearsal the day before the ceremony, but she never showed up. Police found that all of her belongings were still in the apartment she shared with Elton. Not a single thing was out of place or missing. It was as if she had vanished into thin air.

The cops were still searching for her, but leads were drying up and they were communicating less and less with the family. I knew Elton could tell they were going to give up soon. I silently hoped they would find her body. At least then there would be some degree of closure. Thoughts of what might be happening to her haunted even me, so I couldn't imagine how bad it was for Elton. Gwen was a good person and an even better friend. I wanted to see her alive again, but more than that I wanted her not to be in pain.

We sat in silence for the next few minutes as the town grew closer. We were about a half-mile away when the car began to grind and shudder again. I felt it begin to slow even as I pressed on the gas pedal.

"Welp, there it goes," Elton said dryly beside me.

"Shit," I said, flooring the gas in a last-ditch effort to resurrect the car. It gave one final groan and came to a halt by the side of the road.

Elton looked up at the town ahead. "Looks like we're walking."

I sighed and started to get out of the car. "It sure does."

Elton and I agreed that we should leave most of our stuff in the car and only carry the bare necessities to the town. Hopefully, we would find a ride back to the car in addition to someone who knew out to fix it. He and I each packed a small overnight bag just in case and headed toward the ever-darkening horizon.

As we grew closer, I began to realize just how small the town was. It would probably only take a person ten minutes to walk from one end to the next. In addition to that, it was oddly centralized. Unlike most cities, which stretch out and become thinner as you reach the city limits, this one had a very discernable edge that didn't seem to differ in building size or density compared to the center of the town.

Even more oddities became apparent as we approached. The town was *old*. Very old. None of the buildings appeared to have been built after the early 1900s. All were the kind of squat, western-style buildings you'd see in an old movie. Walking into the town was like walking into another century.

The experience became more surreal as we passed the outskirts of the city and began to walk its streets. By now a full moon hung over the horizon and everything was cast in shades of luminous gray. The western aesthetic was even more apparent once you entered the town. Some of the buildings had batwing doors and everything. I felt a chill run down my spine as we explored the town. Something just felt wrong about it. It almost felt like a theme park of sorts or some kind of immersive exhibit. It just didn't feel like a place where people lived. It seemed constructed for aesthetic rather than habitation.

"Do you think it's abandoned?" I asked Elton.

"That would make sense since it wasn't on the map." He scrutinized the buildings around him. "But that can't be right. Everything here is perfectly intact. No chipped paint, no broken doors or windows."

I glanced around and saw that he was right. If anything, the town was too perfect. The windows were all perfectly clean, without a speck of grime on them, something you don't see often in the middle of a desert. The doors and porches were spotless too. Everything looked like it had never been used or even exposed to the elements. My feeling of unease became stronger.

"It doesn't seem like anyone's around," Elton said.

I nodded. The town appeared to be completely empty, although it was well maintained. Perhaps everyone was asleep in bed. People tended to go to bed early in these parts I supposed. However, I noticed that there wasn't a single car in sight. These people couldn't possibly survive without transportation.

We continued toward the center of town. It was at that point that I noticed how eerily quiet the whole place was. Not just the lack of people, but the lack of animals or insects. Everything was utterly silent, void of any life or motion.

As if the town had heard my thoughts, a cacophony of noise exploded around me. Birds tweeted, crickets chirped, and cicadas droned eerily. I nearly jumped out of my skin at the sudden noise. Likewise, Elton gave a short, strangled cry. After the initial surprise, I realized that the abrupt noise hadn't actually been that loud. However, in contrast to the absolute silence that preceded it, the various chirps and calls had seemed deafening. I shot Elton a strange look which he returned.

"Is it just me or was it silent until just now?"

Elton nodded. "It was. Maybe something was scaring the animals into silence."

"What could have done that?"

Elton shrugged and continued toward the center of town. I looked around and listened to the strange cacophony around me. Even more bizarrely, I didn't see a single bird or cricket. No moths or other nighttime insects populated the air either. Despite the sounds of life around us, the world was void of it. It almost seemed that animals intentionally avoided the town in the same way they avoid predators. I shivered at that thought and couldn't help but feel I had walked into the cavernous jaws of a beast.

As we explored further, I noticed more strange aspects of the town. There seemed to be various shops and restaurants scattered about, but the signs that hung above all of them were blank. Not faded or in disrepair, but as if they had never been painted in the first place.

At that point, I looked down and noticed how strange the earth was. The ground looked like sand, but it felt all wrong when I stepped on it. It didn't slide about and run over my feet like loose sand usually does. Rather, my foot sank into it almost like mud.

I knelt and pressed my finger into the sand. Rather than poking a hole in the loose grains, my finger came down on a soft, mesh-like substance that stretched almost like rubber. The ground felt moist and marshy. It was like a sort of foam textured to look like sand.

I stood up and looked to Elton. "Something's not right here," I said. "We should turn back."

Elton shook his head. "The car's broken down. We couldn't go back even if we wanted to."

"Then we'll walk back to the highway and flag down a car. It's only a couple miles out." I gave him a pleading look. "This entire town is just wrong."

"It's a creepy cluster of buildings and nothing more. You're freaking yourself out."

I could tell Elton was scared too. There was a note of unease in his voice that he couldn't mask. But he was being stubborn, always the hardheaded fool. I sighed and turned back to our initial course.

I had only gone a few more steps when I stopped in my tracks. The chatter of nocturnal animals had seemed strange ever since they started. Aside from the suddenness of them and the lack of any visible wildlife, something else had been bothering me, and I finally placed it. The noises around us had a distinct pattern. It was like a recording being played on loop. Two bird chirps there, a cicada drone, several crickets, all playing over and over again. I felt ice run through my veins at the sudden realization.

Elton had gone ahead while I stopped to listen and was now waiting for me to catch up.

"We have to get out of here right now," I said.

"Oh, come on. This is ri-" He was cut off by an enormous groaning sound as the ground shuddered beneath our feet. He went silent and locked eyes with me. We both started running at the same time in the direction we came. The ground continued to shake and the houses around us began to twist and groan. Their wood softened and they seemed to melt along with everything else in the town.

As I sprinted toward where we left the car, I noticed that the ground had become softer. With every step, my foot sank a little deeper until it almost felt like the earth was sucking me in. The ground clutched at my ankles. I began to slow and had to take forceful, jerking steps.

It became increasingly difficult and I was sure I would soon be stuck, but suddenly my foot fell on solid ground. I pulled my remaining leg from the muck behind me and took another step. For a moment I forgot about running and marveled at the feeling of normal earth beneath me. I noticed that I was on the outskirts of town, just past the strict border that defined its edge.

I turned to see that Elton was about fifteen feet behind me. Only, he wasn't moving. He stood completely still.

"Elton," I said, trying to keep my voice from trembling. "Come on!"

"I can't," he said, his voice devoid of emotion. "I'm stuck."

I moved to help but stopped myself. I would get stuck too if I took another step. I watched as he slowly sank further into the ground. The ground began to pull him in even faster and I saw more of him disappear below its surface. He was submerged up to his thighs now.

"I- I'll..." I trailed off. There was nothing I could do. I watched the earth grasp at him like hands clambering up his body.

"Just go," Elton said. "Get away from here, just in case."

I stayed where I was and shot him a stubborn look. I heard him sigh when suddenly his body went rigid.

"What's wrong?"

"I can feel it," he said. His eyes widened and glazed over as if he was looking upon a vast landscape. "I can feel the town like it's part of me." For a moment there was a look of wonder on his face, but then his expression contorted into one of disgust.

"Oh God," he said, struggling to get out. I watched as he thrashed about fruitlessly. "It has roots. It has fucking roots. This is just a part of the whole. There's so much more - entire lakes, mountains, forests, and towns just like this."

This terror lasted only for a moment before it was once again replaced with a kind of surprised awe.

"There are other people here," he whispered. "I can feel them." He was silent for another moment then I heard him gasp. "She's here."

"Who?"

"Gwen," he said. "I can see her. She's here with me. She's been here all along." A look of bliss spread across his face.

The ground was up to his chin now, and I watched in petrified silence as it filled his mouth then pulled him under. His head disappeared below the ground's surface. The town's landscape returned to normal, seemingly as placid and mundane as any other town.

The next thing I remember was running, a mad and frantic dash through the desert with no grasp of in what direction I was headed. I'm not sure how long I ran, but my legs were burning when I finally stumbled upon the highway. Several cars passed and it wasn't long until I was out of that godforsaken desert.

-

I've returned to the Black Rock Desert many times in the past ten years, always searching for that strange little town. But I never found it. There's nothing there except the flat expanse of desert sands. I even managed to find our car, but still, there was nothing on the horizon. Elton was a good man. I hope he really is with Gwen now. But that doesn't change the fact that there are more things like that out there. Strange places where everything is just a little off. Perhaps the shadows point the wrong way, or maybe the trees all grow at strange angles. If you ever find yourself in such a place, trust your instincts and run. Run fast, run hard, and hope to God that it doesn't catch you.

THE TERRORS OF DOCTOR MARROW

Isle was a small, close-knit town. Everyone knew their neighbors, no one locked their doors at night, and they all took care of one another. Furthermore, the town was well off. Harvests were always bountiful, the weather never became too hot or too cold, and no one ever got sick. The last of these blessings was commonly attributed to Doctor Marrow.

The good doctor was a paragon of the townspeople. They looked up to him, respected him, and even revered him. The town had its own government, which Doctor Marrow refrained from participating in. But everyone knew that no decision was ever made without his counsel.

However, a number of oddities surrounded the doctor, though most of the townspeople chose to ignore them. Firstly, no one in the village knew how old Doctor Marrow was. Even the oldest citizen could recall a time or two when they had seen him in their youth. Secondly, he had the odd habit of always wearing dark spectacles that obscured his eyes. Glasses were already difficult to come by in remote villages such as Isle, but ones as ornate and exotic as Marrow's were unheard of. Many people mused that his odd apparel was the most valuable thing in the entire town.

The last of these mysterious traits was his insistence on hosting a celebration every five years. This festival, known as the Giving, encompassed the entire town and gave thanks for their wellbeing. Everyone sang, danced, reveled, and tried to ignore the worrisome thoughts that nagged at them on those strange nights.

It was on this night that the town celebrated the largest Giving they ever had. Doctor Marrow had been particularly excited about this one, claiming that it marked an anniversary of some sort. Isle was ablaze with torchlight and activity. Great food carts were set up in the town square, young women danced as the men cheered them on, and all the craftsmen of the village found some way to turn their trade into a show.

Some of the villagers spent years honing some talent or act just so they could show it off at the Giving. Children made costumes and snuck around trying to scare their peers. For one night, the whole town became a great scene of revelry and fun.

However, every light casts a shadow. The Giving served a greater purpose, one that every townsperson was keenly aware of yet kept locked away in their subconscious. It truly was a terrible thing that happened on those nights. But it was a small price to pay for the wellbeing of the entire village.

In the throes of the night's festivities, Doctor Marrow kept to the shadows. The darkness hung about him like a cloak, seeming to follow him wherever he went. He had no need to hide, for no one in the village would ever dare to accost him, but he found it fitting to remain unseen. As he crept about, his eyes searched behind those dark glasses of his, seeking out his target.

At last, they fell upon a young boy. The doctor didn't know his name, for names mattered not when it came to his prey. It was always just the girl or the boy. The child wandered about in a dark robe fashioned from an old sack. His Giving costume had clearly been rushed and hung about him loosely, threatening to trip him at any moment.

Doctor Marrow swept up beside the boy and knelt down. Townspeople watched from the periphery of his vision. He knew not if their gazes were accusing, nor did he know if any of those eyes belonged to the boy's parents. A hushed silence fell about that one small area in the festival's crowd. A bubble of tense quietude tucked within the deafening roar of the Giving.

"Hello there," the doctor said.

"Hi," the boy responded, his eyes lighting up at the sight of the doctor. Marrow walked as a god among the people of Isle, and its children viewed him as a sort of hero.

"Are you enjoying the festival?" He asked, his face breaking into a kind smile.

The boy nodded enthusiastically. This was the first time he'd spoken to the doctor in person and he was ecstatic. His parents always talked about how much good Doctor Marrow did for the town.

"You seem like a strong little boy," Marrow said, looking him up and down. "Do you think you could help me with something?"

Once again, the boy nodded enthusiastically, and Doctor Marrow grinned even wider at that. "Why thank you, young man. Follow me, and I'll show you what I need you to do." He held out a hand and the boy took it.

The crowd edged away from the pair as they walked hand in hand. Most of the townsfolk glanced away or pretended not to see them, while a rare few fixed the doctor with a piercing gaze.

"Is this really okay?" Asked a hushed voice in the crowd.

"Quiet down," hissed an older voice. "After all he's done for us, who are we to deny the man his pleasures?"

Doctor Marrow frowned at the overheard conversation. It seemed there was dissent among the townsfolk. He supposed it didn't matter. After all, this was to be the final Giving. His work was almost complete.

A carriage took Marrow and the boy to his property on the outskirts of the town. A soaring stone structure atop a hill served as the doctor's home. It had been a military fort centuries ago, but everyone in the town remembered it as having always belonged to Doctor Marrow.

Upon stepping out of the carriage and seeing this bastion of a home, the boy gasped. Doctor Marrow chuckled at his surprise and continued forward. The boy hesitated and remained by the carriage. Nobody was allowed on the doctor's property, especially children. It was one of Isle's most important rules.

"It's okay," Doctor Marrow said as he turned around and gestured for the boy. "You have my permission."

The child rushed forward and, taking the doctor's hand, they began up the winding steps that led to his house. Night was just falling as they reached the top and went inside.

Doctor Marrow's home was richly furnished and cast in the warm glow of torchlight. The normally cold stone floors were now warm and inviting, and as soon as he entered the boy was assailed by a myriad of savory smells.

"Before your task," Doctor Marrow said, "let's have dinner." He guided the boy to a dining hall that contained a table long enough to accommodate at least thirty people. On it was a feast of massive proportions, much unlike anything the boy had ever seen. His face lit up at the sight of it.

"Can I have all of it?" The boy asked.

"You can have as much as you like."

Doctor Marrow sat next to the boy at the end of the table as he tore at the feast ravenously. He sipped from a glass of wine as he watched. The table was laden with all kinds of foods, many of which could never be found near Isle. The boy's face glowed with delight every time he tried something new that he liked, though there was the occasional retching as he tasted some of the more pungent dishes.

The boy's eating slowed until eventually, he stopped altogether. Doctor Marrow hadn't touched a morsel of food the entire time. He looked the boy up and down for a moment and seemed to ponder.

"You're rather dirty after the festival."

The boy glanced down at himself and noticed a few smudges of dirt on his arms and face. Dust coated the tattered edges of his costume. He nodded.

"I think it's best if you take a bath before you help me. I wouldn't want you getting the house dirty."

The boy once again nodded, and he was led from the dining room to another small chamber with a tub in the middle. It was already filled with steaming water and a large fireplace kept the room comfortably warm. A clean, white pair of clothes was folded up near the base of the tub. The doctor gestured to it.

"Those clothes are for you when you're done. I'll leave you to your business now." He closed the door, leaving the boy alone with his bath.

The child stripped down and clambered into the large tub. The bath was relaxing, but he tried not to take too long. He didn't want to disappoint Doctor Marrow after all he had done for the town.

The doctor was waiting patiently just outside the door when the boy finished. He came out wearing the clean white linens given to him by the doctor. The boy never wondered how those clothes had gotten there in the first place, nor did he consider how they managed to fit so perfectly.

"I see you're nice and clean now," Marrow said, looking the boy up and down behind his dark spectacles. He began to walk down the corridor and gestured for the boy to follow.

A few moments later they exited the house through a back door. The boy could see that they were now on the side of the hill that faced away from the town. Doctor Marrow sat in the grass and the boy followed suit.

There was another tall hill directly across from them with a valley in between. The boy noticed what seemed to be a strange cluster of trees in the valley below, but it was too dark to see them clearly. He squinted to try and get a closer look. They looked strange somehow. Too many perfect curves. There was an odd sort of symmetry to them.

"Do you know what tonight is?" Doctor Marrow asked, breaking the silence.

"The Giving." The boy said, though he was not entirely sure if this answer was what the doctor wanted.

Doctor Marrow nodded. "You're right. However, that's not all. You see, tonight is also a full moon and a special one at that. The stars have aligned in a very specific way, and your world teeters on a precarious edge."

The boy nodded, though much of what the old man

said was lost on him.

"You have parents, I suppose." The doctor said.

The boy nodded once again.

"You're not a bastard, are you?"

"No," he replied.

"That's good, child. I too have parents, though I haven't spoken to them in eons. You see, I was a bastard. Of course, my mother preferred the term *abomination*. In the face of her disgust, my father had no choice but to cast me out. I've been in this desolate place ever since."

The boy said nothing in response. It seemed the doctor was lost in thought, talking to himself more than anything. He stared into the sky as if seeing something beyond its vast emptiness.

"Perhaps it would have been better if you were a bastard," Doctor Marrow mused. "It would have been poetic in a sense. I think my father would have liked it."

The boy was becoming anxious. Though he understood little of what the doctor spoke of, an ominous message lurked behind his words. He tried to edge away from the old man, and, as he glanced over, he had the distinct impression that something much larger than Doctor Marrow's frame sat beside him on the grass. It was as if the doctor's body was merely some diminutive shadow of a greater whole.

"Oh well, it can't be helped now." Doctor Marrow got to his feet. "The time is upon us."

As he said those words, the swollen orange body of a full moon edged its way over the hill. Its glow illuminated the valley before them, and the boy gasped in horror.

The land below was barren of any life. What the boy had mistaken for a tangle of trees was something much more gruesome. A great figure stood there with its arms spread. The towering effigy must have been at least a hundred feet tall as the tips of its outstretched hands nearly crested the hills around it. Gargantuan wings sprouted from the figure's back, and the strange leathery material that comprised them flapped limply in the breeze. It was as if a great angel stood there gazing at the sky.

A second wave of horror came when the boy realized what the thing was made of. Its sharp angular body was comprised of bones, all jumbled together in a soaring mockery of the human figure. They were in various stages of decay, as some were bleached white while others still had scraps of flesh hanging from them. The wings were made of skin of all different shades and colors, stitched together like a giant, revolting quilt.

"Do you like my work?" Doctor Marrow asked, staring down at the thing. "After all, I have only you to thank. For many years your village has provided me with the materials I need to complete this piece."

The boy desperately wanted to run, but something held him there. There was a great weight upon his shoulders, pressing him into the ground.

"Perhaps this will convince my father of my worth. I do believe he'll like it."

Doctor Marrow looked down at the boy and grinned. "And with you, it will finally be complete."

The doctor removed his dark spectacles and the boy felt as if his blood had turned to ice. There were no eyes behind those glasses, just two great holes with a terrifying vastness behind them, as if the entirety of the cosmos had been stuffed into Doctor Marrow's skull. The darkness inside swirled and the boy felt himself transfixed, drawn into some cold and dreamless sleep.

THE LABYRINTH

My dearest Emily,

Please, I beg of you to read this letter in its entirety. I don't expect you to forgive me or even respond. I expect no pity from you after what I did. But please read what I have to say. I must at least try to make you understand why I did the things I did.

I'm sure you've figured out by now that something happened in Alaska. I also have no doubt that you've been plagued by a myriad of suspicions ever since. I hope to put those suspicions to rest. You may not believe what I have to say henceforth. Even I find it quite unbelievable at times. But I swear this to be the truth as I know it.

First, I truly mean it when I tell you that I left with only the best of intentions. As you know, I had spent the past several months looking for a job after being laid off, and I was turned down everywhere I went. It seemed like there was no hope. All I wanted was enough to support the two of us. I wanted to live in a nice little house with just me and you, some pets, and maybe even children one day. Yet, with every passing day, it felt as if those dreams were being crushed into the mud.

That is why, when Alex told me about his logging gig in Alaska, I barely gave myself time to think before agreeing to go. But I fear I wasn't entirely truthful with you about the job. The company Alex worked for was desperate for help. They had anticipated being in the forest for three months. But, as the end of the second month approached, they fell increasingly short of their quota.

They lost a man practically every day. Their crew was riddled with accidents, injuries, and more than a few deaths. The more superstitious crewmembers left without warning after complaining of strange sounds and shadows in the night. As the end of their stay grew near, the company saw bankruptcy looming on the horizon. They hadn't harvested nearly as much timber as they'd anticipated and were unlikely to even break even.

They were behind schedule, short on employees, and hemorrhaging money. Alex told me that I could just show up and there'd be no questions asked. The logging company couldn't pick and choose at this point. Additionally, I was promised hefty pay at the end of the month so long as they met their goals.

That's why I left so suddenly after giving you only the barest of explanations. I hoped that you would understand. I never anticipated the terrible things I would face there. If you've read this far, then I beg you to continue. I just need you to understand.

After my flight landed, it wasn't long before I found the logging site. It was located in a dense patch of forest not far from the airport. I remember finding it strange how close we were to civilization yet how isolated it felt under those dark canopies.

Alex greeted me there and introduced me to those running the site. The boss's name was Maxwell. He was gruff and seemed panicky, as if at any moment he expected to get caught doing something he shouldn't. However, as Alex had anticipated, they were happy to have me and cared not for my experience. At the end of the day, manpower was manpower, and they needed all the help they could get.

For the first couple of weeks, I was trained in the basics. They tried to keep me away from the dangerous stuff, preferring to give me menial tasks that they didn't have time to focus on. I spent most of my days running tools from one place to another or helping with organizational work.

However, it wasn't long before I realized the truth about the project. It was an illegal job. We were logging on protected native lands, and that's why everyone was in such a rush to get it over with. The longer we were there, the greater our chances of being caught.

I should have left right then. I didn't want to be involved in something as immoral as tearing down trees on protected land. But I kept thinking of you, Emily. And I couldn't help but imagine what we could do with the payout once my time there was done. So, I kept quiet and did as I was asked. If only I knew what next awaited me in that dark forest.

I'd been there for about a week when Alex approached me and thrust a can of bright orange spray paint into my hands. He instructed me to go into the forest and mark trees to be cut down. I had previously been taught what kind of trees to look for and could determine if the size and quality of the timber were up to their standards. I nodded and made my way into the woods.

The forest was incredibly dense, and thick foliage muffled any sounds I made. Another thing about the forest was that everything seemed wet. The air was humid regardless of temperature and the ground squished beneath my feet as I walked.

As I made my way through the dense shrubbery, I fell into a sort of rhythm. I'd mark a tree, spin around to check those nearest, and, seeing none that were suitable, move on to another batch. It was soothing in a way, being able to focus on a singular task and forget about my worries for at least a moment. I moved through the forest in a trance-like state.

Eventually, a loud birdcall brought me back to reality. I wondered briefly what kind of bird it was. The sound was unlike anything I had ever heard before. Suddenly aware of my surroundings, I realized that I had no idea where I was. I had completely lost my sense of direction and all the trees looked the same to me.

I didn't panic. I had been warned what to do in this situation. I would be able to follow the markings I'd made back to the camp. Some were few and far between, but they wouldn't be too difficult to find.

I started in the direction from which I had come but couldn't find any of the trees I'd marked. Undeterred, I headed in the opposite direction and started to look there. Still, I saw none of the marked trees. They shouldn't have been hard to find. It was bright orange paint in an otherwise green forest.

I became frantic as I moved from tree to tree, circling all the way around each one before moving to the next, desperately looking for one I'd marked. I was just about to give up when I tripped over something solid that protruded from the ground. After standing up and brushing myself off, I saw that it was a block of stone, perfectly flat on every side. I noticed that there were more of them lined up in a path that led off into a cluster of trees.

A wave of relief hit me. Carved stone meant there were people nearby. They created a sort of trail that led into a dark patch of trees and I followed them. I noticed that all of the stones were perfectly cut and exactly the same size. There didn't seem to be much erosion on them, so I figured they hadn't been there too long.

As I followed them, the forest grew even denser. It seemed like I was moving in the opposite direction of where civilization might be, and I considered going back. But seeing that I was already lost, I figured I might as well follow the stones. I could always turn around and follow the same trail back.

I had been trudging through dense shrubbery for a concerning amount of time when I finally came upon a clearing. The stone path terminated just as I stepped out of the tree coverage and into a strange, barren circle. There was an odd hole in the ground several feet in front of me. I moved to examine it and saw that it was some kind of shaft with stairs leading down it. I wondered if this was some strange remnant of a coal mine. Going against my better instincts, I decided to explore it.

The steps descended for a while before I found my-self in a corridor. The walls were smooth and straight, manmade without a doubt. It was dark so I fished a flash-light out of my back pocket and turned it on. I could see that the tunnel stretched on for a while, fading into black-ness in the distance. Several passages branched off from the main tunnel.

By that point, I had realized that it was unlikely there were any people down there, but curiosity got the better of me and I decided to explore further. Something about the tunnels seemed odd, and I couldn't tear myself away from them. It felt as if I had been led there, like something had been nudging me along from the moment I first stepped foot into the forest.

I continued through the tunnels, taking turns at random. I tried to remember the path I had taken so I could eventually find my way back, but it was like trying to grasp water. The more I tried to hold onto them, the faster the memories slipped away. I realized what was happening, but for some reason, I didn't care. The tunnels were the only thing that mattered.

I'd been down there for nearly an hour and hadn't seen any sign of people or even animals. Everything was bare dirt, completely undisturbed. No footprints or objects were scattered about. It seemed the tunnels had laid untouched for decades, but that couldn't have been right. The strange subterranean corridors were in perfect condition, unaffected by erosion and the passage of time.

I turned a corner and stopped dead in my tracks. A figure stood at the end of the corridor illuminated by my flashlight. I could just barely make it out.

"Hey," I said, moving forward. "I'm sorry, I didn't realize anyone was down here." The figure stood still as I continued toward them. I came closer, and finally, it came into sharp focus. I froze.

The thing at the end of the tunnel wasn't human. Its body seemed human enough, but its head was a different story. A ram's head sat atop its torso and watched me, unblinking. Additionally, two horn-like projections curved upwards from its abdomen. They seemed to compliment the ones on its head.

For a moment I tried to convince myself that it was some kind of strange statue. An effigy made by local kids to scare people. But then I saw its chest rise and knew it to be breathing. The creature took a step forward.

I bolted in the other direction, my feet pounding against the soft earth beneath me. I took turns at random, hoping to outmaneuver the thing that lumbered after me. But every time I looked back, I saw it there, following, always just a little closer. I ran and ran and ran, gasping for breath.

I heard it gaining on me. The soft sound of its footsteps matching my own, growing louder with every passing moment. My legs began to burn, and I slowed down. But the thing never seemed to get tired. It kept up the same pace until it was upon me.

I felt the sharp pain of its strange abdominal projections piercing through my back. I tried not to look but couldn't help myself and saw them tear out of my front, blood gurgling up around the wounds. I felt my feet leave the ground and hung there, limp, like a worm skewered on a hook. The creature set me down and withdrew its horns. I fell to the ground and everything faded to black.

I woke up in the tunnels. Suddenly remembering everything that had happened, I reached for my chest where the thing's horns had pierced through me. My clothes were intact and there was no blood. Still not convinced, I ran my hand under my shirt only to feel smooth, unblemished skin underneath.

My head hurt and I felt groggy. I figured I must have either passed out or fallen asleep shortly after coming down there. The ram creature had just been a dream. I shivered at the thought of it. Everything had been so vivid. I could still feel the burning sensation of the creature's horns piercing through me. The white, hot terror as it pursued me through the dark tunnels.

I fumbled around until I felt my flashlight beside me

and flicked it on. I groaned as I stood up. My whole body hurt. I decided to wander around until I found a way out of the labyrinth. That's how I had begun to think of it. As a winding labyrinth not meant to be escaped.

I once again began to wander its winding passages. My dream had been so vivid that I had no idea where reality ended and the dream began. Consequently, I wasn't sure how long I'd been down there before I lost consciousness. I began to feel hopeless as I made my way through tunnel after tunnel.

I felt an eerie prickling sensation on the back of my neck just before I turned down another passage. As soon as I rounded the corner I realized why. The figure was there again, its ghastly, yellow animal eyes gazing at me without a hint of emotion. The fur of its head was matted down and I realized just how strongly the thing smelled. It was like standing next to a rotting corpse. Only sheer terror kept me from retching.

This time I didn't pause to think. I reacted instinctively, turning on my heel and sprinting in the direction I had come from. I heard the thing start after me. Once again it kept pace with me, the sound of its footsteps and heavy breathing mere feet behind me at all times.

I ran until I couldn't anymore, until my chest heaved with the effort and my legs trembled beneath me. Then, just like before, the thing caught up. I felt it tear into me once again and watched as its horns protruded out my front. I hung limply from them, then it pushed me off and I fell to the earth. I felt my mouth fill with blood and watched it splatter on the cold dirt beneath me. Then everything, once again, faded to black.

I woke up in the darkness of the labyrinth again. Like before, I scrambled to check myself for wounds then breathed a sigh of relief when there were none. At that point, I was still naïve enough to believe that it hadn't been real. I convinced myself that it had been a dream within a dream. I flicked on my flashlight and got up, intent on finding a way out.

Then I met the thing again, and again, and again. It didn't matter what path I took. I'd eventually turn a corner and it would be standing there, its yellow eyes gazing at me. Every time I ran away. I ran until it felt like my heart would give out. And every time it caught me.

This became a haunting and inescapable cycle. I would wake up somewhere in the labyrinth, try to find my way out, then eventually be killed by the creature. I had trouble grasping the reality of the situation. Were the past iterations dreams or had I actually lived them and been resurrected? Did it really matter? Regardless, it felt like I lived every single one of those days. I remember every encounter, every moment of searing pain, every death. I lived and died a thousand lives in the labyrinth.

I tried to keep track, but I eventually lost count of how many times I'd encountered the creature. All I knew was that it kept happening, over and over. I became exhausted, endlessly repeating the same actions and ending up the same way. There was no escape. Even the pain and terror became monotonous.

Then something changed. I woke up in the labyrinth as usual. I had stopped checking myself for wounds long ago. Everything had become ritual by that point. Slowly, I stood up and turned on my flashlight. I was weary. I no longer even felt fear anymore. I only wanted the cycle to end.

I wandered the tunnel for about an hour, slowly, leisurely. I wasn't looking for a way out. But the thing would find me regardless, so I figured I would at least stretch my legs. Maybe this time things would be different. Though deep down I knew they wouldn't.

I turned the corner and there it was, stock-still as always, just waiting for me to run. This time I didn't. Previously I had always run, hidden, or, at the very least, walked in the other direction. This time I approached the creature. It wasn't a courageous act. It was a weary one.

I expected it to look confused when I approached. But it didn't react in any way. It just stood there, breathing heavily and watching me. I kept moving forward, barely even aware of what was happening at that point. I just wanted it to be over.

I embraced the creature. I felt its sickle-like horns enter me as I pulled it close. It hurt, but I didn't care. I just needed things to be over. I was so tired. Blood pooled around my feet as I stood there with a monster in my arms. To my surprise, the thing embraced me back. It leaned in and I heard a deep raspy voice.

"Good."

I woke up in the forest to the sounds of men calling my name. My head pounded and my vision swam. I couldn't seem to get a bearing on my surroundings. Remembering the labyrinth, I frantically looked around. I was in a clearing, but the stones and tunnels I remembered seeing before were gone, though that felt like a lifetime ago.

"Here!" I shouted weakly.

Alex was the first to find me. He burst into the clearing and his face broke into a massive grin when he saw me.

"What are you doing all the way out here?" He asked. "We've been looking for you for hours. You're miles from the site."

All I could do was shake my head and shrug. "I'm not sure."

After that incident, the crew quickly wrapped up the logging job. It seemed everyone wanted to be out of there as quickly as possible. They noticed that I had changed. I was a shell of my former self, and it unnerved them.

-

Emily, that shell is what came back to you. Life just felt empty to me after all that. In some ways it felt like I was still in the labyrinth, repeating the same day over and over. Nothing changed for me. Everything was gray. That's when the drinking and drugs started. I needed to escape.

After I drove you away, I started trying to research what happened to me. I don't have any definitive answers, but I think I found a clue. There's a native tribe in that part of Alaska with some unusual lore. It's not well known, but I did some digging and managed to find a few articles about it. There's a man, Dr. Pengloss, who seems to have done a considerable amount of research into their mythology. I tried contacting him but never received a response.

However, I read some of his papers and found that their legends speak of an ancient forest spirit. It seeks out virtuous men and breaks them. It thrives on the degradation of things that are good. It tortures them until they're mere shadows of their former selves. I know you won't believe me. I know it's a stretch. But I swear I'm telling you the truth.

I'm going back there now. I'm going to find proof of what happened to me. Then you'll see that it's not my fault. I'm not a bad man. Something made me this way.

I'll try to fix things, and then we can have the life we always wanted.

I love you, Emily.

This letter was recovered from a body found on protected land just outside of Seldovia, Alaska. The victim was a John Doe. The body appears to have been gored by some animal. Wounds cannot be attributed to any of the known native wildlife. An unknown species or illegally harbored non-native animal is suspected. After a two-week investigation, and with no leads, this case was closed.

-Seldovia Police Department

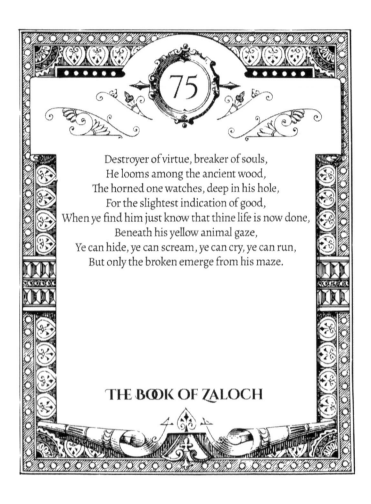

75

Destroyer of virtue, breaker of souls,
He looms among the ancient wood,
The horned one watches, deep in his hole,
For the slightest indication of good,
When ye find him just know that thine life is now done,
Beneath his yellow animal gaze,
Ye can hide, ye can scream, ye can cry, ye can run,
But only the broken emerge from his maze.

THE BOOK OF ZALOCH

THE GREATEST CONQUEROR

The people gathered in the church, black attire abundant, shrouds across their faces, and tears shining in their eyes. They muttered in their little circles, reminiscing and laughing laughs that didn't quite reach their bellies, hollow sounds that failed to fill the silence that hung about the pews. It seemed the loss had left an eternal emptiness by their sides, a great hole in their lives that could never be filled.

The chorus sang and the ceremony began. The people sat when they were supposed to sit and stood when they were supposed to stand. They sang and prayed and knelt. The priest did as he had always done and tried to ignore the tears in the parishioners' eyes. The mass went on as usual until a shadowed figure made its way up the aisle in gloomy silence.

A man stood at the pulpit, his hair disheveled and bags heavy beneath his eyes. He spoke of the lost one between chokes and sobs. The crowd nodded along with his words, smiling when he spoke of fond memories, frowning when he choked up. Their faces screwed into an expression of sympathy, or perhaps, in some, one of disgust for the weakness of the man before them.

Eventually, the speech turned from one of grief to one of hope. The man spoke of life after death, of a great savior, and of God above. He spoke of a good life lived by the deceased and ensured the audience that they would be reunited with their love if they too lived well. Those in the pews smiled at that and tried to look as if there was hope still in their hearts.

But, deep down, they knew that death had won, as it always does. They knew that the final victor, the greatest conqueror, had its way once more. It stood as a towering god among them, and they lived their entire lives in its shadow. This truth sank deep into their bones and chilled them to their very souls. It lay heavy upon them, and they carried this weight with them wherever they went.

With this solemn truth carved into their very hearts, the mournful crowd concluded the mass and began the solemn procession to the graveyard. They sat in silence in their cars as the hearse made its way through midday traffic. Once there, the lost one was lowered into the ground while those above continued to rattle on about eternal life and death beaten into submission. However, these words fell hollow, and even the most naïve of mourners knew the terrible truth that comes at the end of every life: death was always the victor.

As dirt was piled atop the casket, there came a second ceremony. A great writhing began within the earth, unbeknownst to those above. There was no talk of hope or salvation. Nor was there any talk of death. There was only the final, mindless conquerors. It happened slowly but with great hunger. The worms had arrived at last. They came. They saw. They ate.

THE REALITY CONTAGION

Jason Kember and his mother never had what one would call a healthy relationship. While Jason had always preferred the cold, precise world of logic, his mother favored her own realities founded in mysticism and the occult. As one would expect, this led to a great schism between the two. Jason would look on in disdain as his mother fiddled with her silly Tarot cards or tried to commune with the stars. He instead elected to dissect his world beneath the scalpel of reason, leaving it shamelessly revealed, innards and all.

Once, Jason's mother came home from the grocery only to bring in bag after bag of white rice. When Jason, fourteen at the time, asked her why, she claimed that a dream had instructed her to. Despite their waning finances and the constant stream of overdue bills that flooded the mailbox, she refused to return the countless bags of grain. So, they ate only rice for months after that, day after day, night after night.

Moments like those were a defining characteristic of Jason's childhood. At first, his mother confused and even scared him. Then, as he grew older, he began to pity her. Then his pity grew thin, and he found himself resenting her ridiculous antics and complete disregard for responsibility. His father had left when he was young, and rather than hating him as he had in the past, he began to empathize with the old man. His mother lived in her own reality, separate from the reality of others and the responsibilities it brought. She became an exhausting and unbearable presence.

-

Now, at the age of twenty-five, Jason lived six-hundred miles away. He had a car, a steady job, a nice apartment, and, most importantly, no need for his mother. She had begun to dabble in occult rituals, trying to see things that don't exist. And as her beliefs and actions became more convoluted, he stopped talking to her altogether. In the past five years, he had only spoken to her twice. Or at least that was the case until recently.

Two weeks ago, Jason received a strange call in the middle of the night. He awoke to the sound of his phone blaring from the nightstand and quickly answered, thinking it was an emergency. It was only his mother. She was babbling something about how the sky was getting smaller. It was growing ever closer, slowly strangling the earth in shadow, until eventually we would be crushed by an ever-advancing net of darkness.

Jason hung up. He had little patience for his mother's antics and even less for nonsense. He made a mental note to call her in the morning and tried to go back to sleep. But she called again, and again, and again. Over and over, endless babble of things unseen and things unknown.

It was at that moment he realized that she had become completely unhinged. A good son may have tried to comfort her or at the very least contacted a mental health professional. But Jason did none of those things. He simply blocked her number and went back to sleep.

The next couple of days were perfectly normal. No random calls, no babble, only the blissful peace of his regular routine: breakfast, work, TV, sleep, repeat. One would think that ignoring his mother would weigh on Jason's conscience. But it didn't. He had simply put it out of his mind. His mother had never treated him as her responsibility, why then would he treat her as his?

On the third day, he received yet another call, this one from an unknown number. He stared at the phone for a moment and chewed his lip thoughtfully. With a sinking feeling in his stomach, he answered it. His mother was on the other end. She had apparently gotten a new phone or was using someone else's. He moved to hang up, but stopped, deciding to hear her out if only for a moment.

"Jason?" Her voice was clear. Much more lucid than the times before, without the frantic rush of words he was accustomed to.

"Yes," he said, unsure how else to respond.

"Please don't hang up," she said. "I'm sorry about my previous calls. I'm better now, more conscious in a way."

He hesitated. She seemed coherent, more so than she'd been in years. Going against his instincts, Jason decided to listen to her. "It's okay. What happened? You seemed out of control."

"I was," his mother responded. "I performed a ritual, one I never should have done, and I saw something terrible. I think what I saw is still inside me somehow."

As she spoke, Jason felt his heart begin to sink. She was just as crazy as always. "Are you okay now?" He was suddenly eager to get this call over with.

"I'm…not sure. I think so, but it feels as if there's still something inside me, writhing, searching for a way out."

He shook his head and sighed. "Well, let me know if that thing inside you acts up again, I guess. I have to go now. Bye." He ended the call before she could respond.

Jason assumed that would be the end of it. He figured that his mother, in her old age, simply had a senior moment and was now back to her less than usual self. He returned to his normal life and seemed content with the way things were. That contentment lasted until three hours later when his phone rang once again.

"Jason," the voice on the other side hissed. There was no lucidity this time, no true thought. Only the frenzied speech of one who thinks they're privy to some cosmic secret and is desperate to communicate what they've seen.

Jason didn't respond, but his mother continued, nonetheless. "I've seen the truth, child. The reality that lies beyond the meager shadow of our own. The invisible dark and twisted things that curl about our mundane world. The horrors that are awakening, within and without, the aspects of the broken one that hunger for us."

"*Shut. Up.*" Jason enunciated each word with cold precision. The icy disdain in his voice stopped his mother's drivel. "I am sick of your nonsense. I spent my entire life listening to your constant talk about mysterious forces and worlds unseen. We're done."

With that, he hung up. He waited for the phone to ring again, rage still heavy in his gut, eager for another opportunity to come roaring forth. But the phone remained silent. Eventually, Jason's anger faded to mild irritation, then to nothing at all.

But still, a deeper emotion gnawed at him. At first, he thought it was annoyance at his mother. But, no, that didn't seem right. The feeling stayed there throughout the evening, churning within him. Like the thing his mother claimed writhed within her, it tossed and turned inside him all evening. It wasn't until late that night, as he was drifting off to sleep, that he realized what it was. The heavy sensation deep within him was concern for his mother.

The next day he decided to do something about her mental state. For the past few years, he had toyed with the idea of putting her in the care of a psychiatric institution. However, due to a combination of apathy and lack of funds, he never had. However, he was considerably more stable now and figured doing so would at least keep her from calling him all the time.

Several days later, he found a good facility, Hurston Psychiatric Clinic, and provided an explanation of his mother's erratic behavior to the professionals there. She had called him several times since then, always babbling about the things she sees, and Jason had recorded her calls. He presented them to the clinic, and they agreed that she should be taken into their care.

That was how he found himself returning home for the first time in years. It was the day his mother was to be transported to the clinic. He had caught a flight, rented a car, and was now mere moments away from a most unwelcome reunion. He arrived fifteen minutes before the people from Hurston were supposed to get there.

That was when the chaos began. Jason had only taken his first step up the driveway when he heard a shriek from the doorway.

"Stay back!" His mother stood on the other side of a screen door, little more than a silhouette, a pale imitation of the woman she had been before. He was several yards away, but Jason could see that she had become stick thin. She looked unbalanced and frail, but not in the way of a sickly person. Though shrouded by the screen, something about her form was wrong. It was as if she had been shifted internally, though not in a physical sense. As if her *essence* had been yanked about and now hung limp around her like rags from a mummy.

Jason shook the irrational thoughts from his head and continued forward. He wouldn't let his mother's absurdities prey upon him. The moment he took another step her shouts rang out again.

"Don't come any closer!" She sounded frantic, worried even. "It'll get you too. I can't keep it inside me."

Jason sighed but decided to humor her. "Can't keep what inside of you?"

"The truth. The cruel reality that exists beyond this one. The twisted union of things formed and unformed. The undoing has begun, and they come to observe and laugh as we are unmade. The ones that watch the watchers and all who see beyond…" She trailed off as Jason grew closer at which point she began to panic. His mother no longer tried to speak and only breathed quickly and unevenly, each breath raspier and more ragged than the one before.

He realized that this was going to be more difficult than he thought. Jason held out his hands in a calming gesture. "It's okay mom," he said as he reached for the door handle. "Everything's going to be fine."

For a brief moment her gaze softened, and it appeared that clarity had overcome her. But, just as quickly as it appeared, the expression was replaced by sheer terror and panic.

"No!" She screeched as she grabbed the screen door from the inside and put all her weight into holding it closed. Jason tried unsuccessfully to jerk the door open.

His mother was surprisingly strong. He sighed and stepped back, putting his hands up once again in a sign of surrender.

"Okay, I won't come inside."

She searched his face for a moment. Despite her incoherence, she still seemed keen in a way. She had yet to lose all of her sensibilities. Seeing that he seemed to be telling the truth, she relaxed her grip on the door, though she still held it loosely.

Jason actually was telling the truth. He wasn't going to come into the house. However, he never said anything about the two burly men from Hurston who showed up clad in white uniforms several minutes later.

She screamed, fought, and generally resisted the whole process, but the two men were experienced with this sort of thing and made short work of getting her into the van. By the time they closed the vehicle door she had calmed down a bit and now sat pouting in silence, occasionally darting a wicked glance at Jason.

He got back into his car and followed them to the psychiatric center. It was only an hour away, and the time passed rather quickly. Jason mentally calculated what the monthly cost of his mother's treatment would be. He sighed. It was more than he liked, but it would keep her out of his hair and hopefully help her in the process.

"She remained quiet the entire ride," one of the men informed him as he got out of his car at Hurston. "It seems she's calmed down for the most part."

Jason nodded and approached where his mother sat in the back of the van. "Come on," he said. "It's time to go inside."

She narrowed her eyes. "I can't believe you would do this. You always were an ignorant child."

Jason exploded at his mother's words. "*I'm* the ignorant one? Do you actually believe that?" He shouted and gesticulated wildly. The van's driver shot him an odd glance, but Jason was too angry to notice. "You're the one who has always refused to use even a modicum of logic! I have suffered my whole life because of your silly beliefs and need to feel so goddamn special all the time."

Jason grew silent after that. He was breathing heavily and staring intently at his mother as he waited for her to respond. She didn't say anything for a long moment, choosing instead to stare at him with a complete and total lack of emotion.

Finally, she spoke. "You've doomed everyone here," she said. "Even now I feel it reaching out of me, grasping for anything and everything it can get its hands on. I should have raised you better."

Jason was prepared to respond, but the flat, icy quality of his mother's voice left him speechless. There was no emotion in that voice, neither anger nor panic, just cold, simple acceptance, as if what she said was neither a threat nor a warning but merely a statement of fact. And with that statement hanging in the air, Jason and his mother were ushered inside where he signed paperwork and followed as she was shown to her room.

After that, Jason was assured by an employee that everything would be okay, and he was free to leave whenever he liked. Satisfied that his mother was taken care of, Jason left and drove back to her house. He had decided to stay there for the next few days until his mother settled into her new accommodations. The house looked as it always had, small and cluttered. Jason had few fond memories there, but still, there was a hint of nostalgia and with it a small amount of comfort.

Things were uneventful the next day. Jason cleaned the house a little and found that his mother had amassed an extensive collection of candles, cards, herbs, and other occult paraphernalia. It seemed every spare cent had been dedicated to growing her assortment of supposedly magic items.

Jason sighed as he rifled through the clutter. It was sad to see someone so desperate to escape their reality, always reaching for something more, always trying to be special. She seemed so intent on escaping her mundane life. He supposed many people were like that in a way, it just so happened that his mother resorted to more esoteric methods.

He decided to put all her trinkets in the attic. Finding a cluster of old boxes in a closet, he packed his mother's things away. There was a lifetime of objects to distract her from the world around her, enough to distract her from the crying baby in the next room, or the hungry child playing outside, or the lonely teenager sobbing beneath his sheets, or the silence of an empty house.

Jason was in the middle of carefully packing a box of glass herb jars when his phone rang. He jumped at the sudden noise and nearly dropped the box. He sighed and set it down gently before answering.

"Jason Kember," he answered, always cordial.

"Hi, Jason," the woman on the other end replied. Her voice was pleasant but there was a hurried note in it, professionalism superseded by a deeper worry. "This is Natalie from Hurston Psychiatric Clinic. I hate to bother you, but there's a problem with your mother."

There was a brief pause, as if she was searching for the right words. Jason waited for her to continue.

"She seems to be having an episode. Normally we'd

be able to handle it ourselves, but she's managed to rile up the other patients. They seem to be playing off the things she says. Are you in any position to come here and help calm her down?"

Jason rubbed his temples in frustration. It hadn't even been a full day yet, and his mother was already causing trouble. "Yes of course. I can be there in an hour."

Fifty minutes later he screeched to a halt outside of the clinic. A young blonde woman sat at the desk as he entered.

"Are you Natalie?" He asked, doing his best to keep the frustration out of his voice. He knew it wasn't her fault that his mother was being difficult.

Natalie nodded in response. There were dark circles under her eyes and her hair was in disarray.

"I'm Jason Kember. You called earlier about my mother."

"Oh, good, you're here." She stood up. "Once again, I'm so sorry to bother you, but we're having trouble keeping everyone under control."

"It's fine," he lied. "I'm glad you called."

Natalie led him to a pair of metal doors and passed a card over the scanner next to them. A loud buzz sounded, and she pushed the doors open, leading him into a corridor with rooms on either side.

They walked down the hallway in tense silence. As Jason approached his mother's room, the hallway grew restless with noise. He began to hear patients rambling in their rooms. As he continued further, they began to shout, and in the immediate vicinity of her room, he heard them screaming and throwing themselves against the walls.

Orderlies milled about, trying to calm the patients down. Several gave him a sidelong glance as they passed, but there was nothing behind their eyes. It was as if they were looking through him. Jason didn't know why but he shivered at that.

They arrived at the room that was the epicenter of the chaos. Surprisingly, it was silent on the other side.

"I'll stay out here," Natalie said as she gestured for him to enter. Jason would have liked to believe that she was just giving them privacy, but he detected what seemed to be a hint of fear in her voice. Were these people really afraid of his mother? She was unhinged and perhaps even violent, but she was still just a frail old woman.

When Jason entered the room, he expected his mother to be raving or tearing apart the furniture, perhaps even slamming her head against the wall in a fit of insanity. But she did none of those things. As he stepped over the threshold, she merely sat on her bed in the corner. She didn't glance up at him as he entered. She didn't move at all, just sat there staring at nothing as chaos reigned around her.

Dark circles ringed her eyes and her hair hung loosely about her face. She sat completely still as Jason approached her. He couldn't even tell if she was breathing. The small woman was a terrifying presence in the room, a stone-like figure with infinite capacity for terror and surprise. Despite being much larger and stronger than his mother, Jason felt as if he was in danger. He noticed that her eyes had the same sunken, hollow look as the orderlies. The look was more than that of a tired person. It was that of someone who felt incomprehensibly small in the face of a greater terror, an impending unknown poised to tear apart the very fabric of that which is good.

Jason shook his head and tried to focus on his mother. It was as if a dense fog clouded his mind. He wondered why he had been called here. His mother was quiet. She wasn't present and didn't seem to be coherent in any way, but neither was she affecting the other patients. He felt a sense of irritation at the oversight of the clinic's staff but calmed himself and thought it through. It was likely that she had only calmed down upon his arrival.

"Hey mom," he said, taking a step toward her. She didn't acknowledge him and only continued to sit there, dazed and unfocused. Jason took another step forward and moved to place a hand on his mother's shoulder. Without intending to, his hand stopped inches from her skin. A sudden fear gripped him. If he touched her something terrible would happen. It was stupid. It was illogical. But that thought kept running circles in his head, twisting round and round until it felt like all of his thoughts were out of place. He stumbled back without realizing it.

"Their eyes are being opened." She spoke at last.

"What?"

She nodded her head toward the walls of her room where shouts were audible from patients down the hall. "They scream because it hurts. It's like having your eyes closed your entire life only to open them and find you're staring directly into the sun. It burns. But they'll acclimate soon enough."

"What are you talking about?" Jason asked.

"They've seen the same truth I saw. It's like a sickness. It seeps out of me and into everyone who comes close." She glanced up and stared at Jason. "It's all your fault. I tried to protect them."

Jason remained silent, not knowing what to say. How do you respond to someone who is utterly convinced of something that isn't true and lacks the mental capacity to see that?

"He reminds me of you," she said, breaking the silence once again.

"Who?"

"The object of this horrible truth. He who has shown it to us and who propagates its horrors. You're very much like him, The Vivisector. You've always scrutinized your world, picking it apart with your logic. He too picks apart the world, but not with the intention of understanding it. He does it simply because there's something to take apart, to watch bleed out on the table and writhe in agony. He's begun His work, and we can only pray for anesthesia."

"I know you think what you're saying is true, but you're sick, mom. None of it's real." He wanted to continue, but his words felt hollow and thin. He felt himself toeing the line of her world as his own disbelief began to fade and be replaced by a sort of primal fear.

He went to make a final point, but no words came. Feeling exhausted, shaky, and slightly embarrassed, he left his mother's room without realizing how careful he was to not turn his back to her.

Natalie was outside waiting for him. She seemed to have somehow grown even more haggard in the five minutes he was gone.

"How'd it go?" She asked.

"She wasn't hysterical at all," Jason responded.

"That's strange. She must have calmed down as soon as you got here."

Her speech was a little rushed and she seemed to look anywhere but at Jason. Growing suspicious, he narrowed his eyes and tried to determine if she was telling the truth. After an awkward moment of silence, he relaxed and decided not to push the issue. He was probably just being paranoid after that strange encounter with his mother. The thought of it sent chills down his spine. He tried to chide himself for fearing his own mother, but some deeper part of him whispered that perhaps his feelings were justified. Something was certainly wrong here.

"I have a strange question to ask," Natalie said, her voice a little higher pitched than usual.

Jason waited for her to continue.

"I know this is an odd request, and it violates company policy, but do you think it would be possible for you to stay the night here? Your presence seems to have a calming effect on your mother, and it would help if we could at least give her some preliminary treatments without worrying about the other patients getting riled up."

"Why don't you just sedate her?"

Natalie hesitated to answer, and, in that moment, Jason realized why he had been called here. His mother hadn't been hysterical. They were scared of her. The strange look he had been seeing on the orderlies wasn't just exhaustion. It was fear. Even more than that, it was the despair of not even understanding why you're afraid, haunted by some ancient survival instinct that keeps screaming for you to run.

Jason held up a hand to stop Natalie's response. "I understand," he said. And he did. There was something deeply wrong with his mother and it scared even him.

"Thank you," Natalie said. There was relief in her voice. "Would you like me to show you to your room?"

He nodded and was led out of the hallway. Natalie brought him to an adjacent corridor lined with slightly larger, comfier rooms. She informed him that many of the orderlies lived in the facility, as it was in a remote location and it allowed them to help patients all hours of the day. She showed him to the empty room that was to be his.

He settled in and sat on the bed. There was little to do. He hadn't expected to stay there and didn't even have extra clothes. He shrugged. The clinic might have a uniform he could wear or at least a way for him to wash his current attire.

He thought about his mother and her strange behavior. More than that, he considered the behavior of the orderlies and patients. It was as if everyone had some eerie, subconscious fear response to his mother. Something primal, the way humans naturally find ancient predators like snakes or spiders revolting. He shivered at the thought of it. What about his mother could be making people react this way? It was as if she were some age-old adversary, just barely remembered by our oldest genes.

He thought he glimpsed movement out the corner of his eye and whipped around to face the door. There was nothing there save the flicker of old halogen bulbs. He shook his head and rubbed his eyes. Jason knew he was letting all the chaos of this place get to his head.

After his heart stopped its pounding, he laid down and tried to relax. It was getting late in the evening, and he knew he should probably sleep soon. He got up to turn the lights off and flopped back into bed. The dim flicker of emergency lights in the hallway illuminated his room through the window in his door. Despite his relatively bright surroundings, Jason drifted off into a deep sleep.

A strange banging sound woke him. It was quiet at first, but, as he laid there listening, it began to grow louder. He realized that it was coming from outside. A dark silhouette just barely peeked into view through the narrow window in the door.

He continued to lay in bed, stock-still as his heart pounded against his ribcage. Jason had a sick feeling in his gut. Despite knowing he should investigate the noise, he couldn't bring himself to move an inch.

Only when the sound grew to a pounding that rocked the door in its fame did he muster the monumental effort it took to shed the covers and approach it. The noise sounded as if someone was slamming their body against the other side. Before he could reconsider, he flung open the door.

Someone was standing in the hallway. Their head rocked back and forth as if they were still rapping it against some object. The light was dim, but Jason could see that their hair was red. Slowly, their head bobbed less and less until it came to a complete stop. The person looked up at Jason and he gasped in horror.

It was Natalie. What he thought had been red hair was actually her blonde locks covered in blood. Her forehead was practically shredded, and he thought he could see fragments of bone gleaming bloody in the light.

"It burns," Natalie said, staring at him with empty eyes. Her voice was haggard and void of emotion. She said it more as a statement of fact than a complaint.

Jason almost gagged at the sight but managed to choke it down and respond. "It's okay, Natalie. We're going to take you to a doctor and get you some help." He moved to take her arm.

"No," she said sounding angry. Jason stopped in his tracks. "The knowing and the seeing. It's like a fire. It hurts so bad. But there is healing in it, a greater holiness to His truth. We must find bliss in the knowledge that He is going to tear our world apart and thus become one with him, tools in his hands." She began to moan, a strange sing-song sound that sent chills down Jason's spine.

He wanted to help her, but every fiber of his being screamed at him to get away. He sprinted down the hallway, terror driving him more than any conscious choice. As he ran, he passed more orderlies and patients. They all pounded their heads against the bedroom doors, moaning in a strange chorus punctuated by the crack of bone on wood.

Two more people hung from nooses in the hallway. The same terror that gripped him had driven them beyond the point of madness. He noticed as he passed that the nooses didn't look quite right. They weren't ropes, but black vine-like hands that sprouted from the ceiling and wrapped around their victims' throats.

Jason let out a guttural sound of terror, something between a scream and a sob, and sped up until his legs burned beneath him. The hallway seemed to be impossibly long. No matter how fast he moved or how long he ran, the glowing exit sign at the end never seemed to get any closer. More horrors slid past him on every side, cloaking the walls and ceiling, moaning and screaming in agony or ecstasy.

He tried to think of a rational explanation. Surely there was something that made sense. A disease! That must be the cause. Some airborne pathogen carried by his mother that affects the brain. As he pondered the ramifications of such an illness, he burst through a pair of double doors and into the clinic's lobby.

It was dark. No emergency lights shone in this room and everything was shrouded in darkness. He saw the glow of moonlight through the double doors of the entrance and lurched for it. His hands were inches from the handle when he stopped. He stood completely still for a moment, frozen by something inside him.

It seemed he stared at nothing, or perhaps he stared at everything. Maybe he stared at that which lies between nothing and everything, the dark and endless shadow of our world. He began to moan, a low and horrible sound filled with pain and dawning realization.

"So, you've seen it," a voice said behind him.

He turned to see his mother sitting at the reception-ist's desk. He continued to moan, a horrible, whining sound that grated at his ears. As he looked at her, he saw a shadow rise up behind her. A thing of monstrous propor-tions, a great and terrible purveyor of destruction. It was a darkness that had its own gravity, it writhed and shifted as it drew at everything around it with a terrible power. The Vivisector.

"It's a horrible truth, I know," his mother said. Ja-son's moans turned to something more like a whine, the kind of sound a child might make after being severely in-jured. "It's okay my son. I'm sorry you had to see this." There was a hint of genuine sympathy in her voice, as if her love for Jason managed to just barely peek through, spilling from somewhere beyond that terrible thing behind her.

Jason was crying now. Hot, wet tears ran down his face as he stared at his mother. His eyes burned with them and she swam in his vision. The only thing that remained in focus was the shadow. That fucking shadow.

"There's a way out," his mother said as she held out her arms. A rope was coiled in her hand. It looked snake-like in the dim room. "I can offer you this mercy."

Jason nodded and he felt the blackness grip him. It suffocated him, drawing the air from his lungs and the life from his bones. Everything faded until there was nothing left but the shadow suspended in eternity.

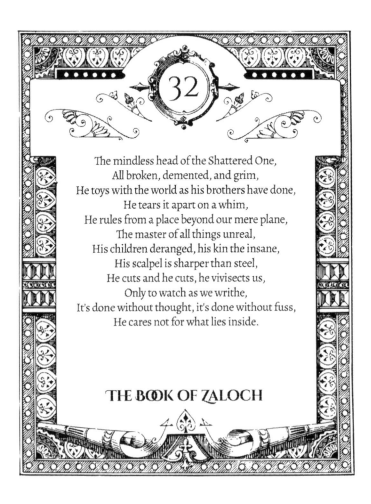

32

The mindless head of the Shattered One,
All broken, demented, and grim,
He toys with the world as his brothers have done,
He tears it apart on a whim,
He rules from a place beyond our mere plane,
The master of all things unreal,
His children deranged, his kin the insane,
His scalpel is sharper than steel,
He cuts and he cuts, he vivisects us,
Only to watch as we writhe,
It's done without thought, it's done without fuss,
He cares not for what lies inside.

THE BOOK OF ZALOCH

THE OAK

Luke was a young and excitable child. Having grown up in a home with ample land, he enjoyed the outdoors more than anything. He loved the sun and the grass and the animals. But, more than that, he loved the trees. One of his favorite pastimes was climbing up a tall and ancient oak so that he could sit and listen to the birds.

His father always warned him not to climb too high. But Luke never heeded his warnings. He was as surefooted and nimble as any child, and his classmates lauded him for how quickly he could scale a tree. However, even the best fail eventually. After attempting to climb to the very top of the oldest and tallest tree in town, Luke fell. His friends recall hearing a shout then gagging as they found him spilled upon the tree's roots.

He was loved by many, and the whole town mourned, but none more so than his father. Luke's father had loved him very much and wanted to do something special to commemorate his resting place. He had heard of a new burial service that allowed one to be buried in a capsule that one day grew into a tree. After much thought, he decided that would be fitting for Luke.

Luke was buried on a cool September day in the center of the town's cemetery. They figured his tree would make a fine centerpiece. There was much crying and the graveyard echoed with the sound of sobs. Everyone knew there was no pain like losing a child.

However, even that tremendous pain faded with time, and Luke's tree grew. The town suffered some harsh winters and the tree struggled at first, but eventually, it grew large enough to withstand the icy winds. Luke's father visited the tree every day, but he soon died, and no one was left to visit the tree.

The tree grew and grew, but as it did a strange phenomenon began to occur. Its roots took on an uncanny red color and an odd knot formed in the trunk. No one noticed these changes save the groundskeeper who had been watching the tree grow for years by then. Sometimes when he glanced at the tree, he couldn't help but think that the face of a child had formed in the trunk. The thought filled him with unease.

One night he was cleaning the grounds when he heard an odd sound coming from the center of the cemetery. He could have sworn it sounded like the tree was wailing. He shook the thought from his head and told himself it was only the wind. He tried to ignore the fact that there was no breeze that night and the grounds were otherwise quiet. The wailing became a regular occurrence for him, and he quickly learned to put it out of his mind.

The cemetery began to lose money until it was no longer able to remain in business. The groundskeeper was laid off and the graveyard was left in disarray. Eventually, the cemetery was forgotten entirely, and foliage grew over the headstones, obscuring the reality of what lay beneath.

But that wailing continued night after night. If one were to walk by, it might sound like someone crying for release from a wooden prison. Or perhaps it was only the wind.

THE GRAY KING

Most people operate under the delusion that dreams are nothing more than hallucinations, fanciful projections of the mind while we remain safe in bed, unaware and unaffected by any of the images we might encounter in our slumber. I once also lived under such blissful pretenses, ignorant to what lay beyond the gateways of slumber. However, at a young age, I was remedied of such beliefs and began to see the truth of dreams.

You see, as a child, I dreamed much more vividly than my peers. I often had what are called *lucid* dreams. I remained aware and in control of them, able to explore and command my slumbering world as I pleased. Bolstered by this freedom, I excitedly went to bed every night, eager to return to a world I preferred over the monotony of reality.

At that point, I still believed that my dreams were nothing more than wholly internal hallucinations. But one night came when I was dissuaded of this misguided belief. I dreamed that I sat on a beach where all the sand seemed to be comprised of diamond dust that glimmered like a rainbow in the setting sun. I enjoyed myself, kicking up the sand and watching how it caught the rays of light as it settled back to the ground.

In addition to the strange granules that littered the shore, a number of odd stones littered the beach. These perfectly spherical rocks looked much like translucent marbles, and each one contained a shimmering spiral, as if a whirlwind had been trapped within it. I was enamored with these strange little stones and liked to set them spinning as the whirlwind inside them twirled round and round.

The next morning, I woke to find a hard object tucked beneath my pillow. Clenched in my fist was one of those stones. I marveled at it in the morning sun as the twister inside seemed to spin with the changing light.

At first, I thought that perhaps I had acquired the stone in the waking world and later dreamed about it. I puzzled over the unusual occurrence for a while but soon forgot about it. However, time and again upon waking I would find an object from my dreams with no explanation as to how it got there. It was always something small and simple: rocks, scraps of paper, strange leaves.

I came to refer to these things as my *souvenirs*, objects taken from the world of dreams and made incarnate in our own. Over time, I realized that they didn't last for long in our world. They just disappeared after a while, and I could never find them again no matter how hard I searched. I supposed they returned to their place of origin, unable to maintain their existence in our world, much like how we are unable to exist in the world of dreams for too long at once.

Eventually, I gained a semblance of control over this ability. I could increase the likelihood of an object appearing in the real world by interacting with it and focusing intently upon it. Additionally, the amount of time an object could exist in our reality decreased as the objects became more complex. Something as simple as one of those pebbles might last for weeks, while something like a book lasted only for an hour before disappearing. I also found that the more complicated objects became bastardized versions of themselves in the real world. An apple in the dream world might become rotten upon coming into ours. I once returned with a book only to find that its pages were suddenly made out of what was almost certainly flesh.

For a long time, this power seemed nothing more than a novelty. It had no real impact on my life, as I could never return with anything complex enough to be of any true value, and my dreamworld contained nothing that could be considered legal tender. My dreams occurred in a wild, fantasy landscape with abandoned castles, boundless forests, and soaring mountains. The dreamworld remained untouched by modern innovations and existed in what seemed to be a state of childlike innocence.

When I was fifteen my father died unexpectedly, and it was then that I saw the terrible power my dreams held. His death traumatized me. The ache of his absence plagued every waking moment of my life. However, it wasn't long before his presence plagued even my dreams.

He was the first human that I had ever seen in my dreams. He walked around aimlessly, unaware of anything going on around him. Usually, he kept to the shadows, as if subconsciously sneaking about. The first few times I saw him, I ran and embraced him. But he paid no attention to me and continued to gawk at things without truly seeing them. Any semblance of intelligence had left him.

This shell of my father scared and saddened me. He haunted me in a way, moving through my dreams like a ghost and trailing me wherever I went. He lurked at the edges of my vision, ignorant of his own actions, as if some external force drove him to follow me.

I can only assume that my constant thoughts of him, both conscious and unconscious, forced him to be attached to me in a way. This attachment appeared to drag his spirit, or at the very least some phantom aspect of him, into my dreams. All of this culminated in a horrendous incident from which I fear I've never truly recovered.

On the night in which it happened, I noticed that my father pervaded my dreams even more than usual. He had been on my mind all day, and this rumination seemed to have bled into my unconscious state. He remained unusually close to me, trailing me wherever I went and nearly bumping into me at times. He was a specter, always at my shoulder.

Without warning, I was torn from my dream by a sound in the waking world. I opened my eyes to see that my father was there, sitting in the corner illuminated by the light of a full moon. He rested on the floor, naked and limp, like a puppet carelessly thrown down by its master. His limbs twisted about at strange angles, and his head hung awkwardly to the side.

As I woke, he turned to face me, and I gasped in horror at the sight. The proportions and placement of his features evoked a deep wrongness. The hollows of his eyes were too large, and his nose was but a slight lump in the middle of his face. Moonlight reflected off his too-smooth skin and his mouth was a mess of twisted flesh. It looked as if an inexperienced artist had attempted to mold my father out of clay and tragically failed.

The thing that was my father tried to speak, but nothing that could be considered words came out of that monstrous mouth. He only made a garbled, rasping noise, and the emptiness in his eyes told me there was no true intelligence behind them. The creature was a gross facsimile of my father cruelly dragged from my sleeping mind. It sat there, twitching and groaning in a bastard tongue.

I nearly screamed at the sight but clasped a hand over my mouth to stop myself. I didn't want my mother to hear and be exposed to the terror sitting in the corner of my room. She was already fragile after the death, and I knew she would never recover from the sight.

The creature continued its unnerving attempts at speech, its eyes swiveling back and forth but never really settling on anything in the room. I watched its crude imitations of human behavior for what seemed like an eternity but couldn't have been more than a minute. At one point I blinked and when I opened my eyes it was gone, unable to maintain its existence in this reality for too long. I breathed a sigh of relief and remained awake for the rest of the night.

After that, I began to fear my dreams. I had seen what terrible power they held, and I became acutely aware of my ability to bring things back without intending to. I stayed awake for several days after, but eventually, my will gave out and I fell into a deep slumber. My father never appeared in my dreams again.

I became conscious of everything I interacted with in my slumber, afraid to bring back anything monstrous as I had with my father. I avoided living creatures in general and even spent much of my time away from the forests I often frequented. I remained in open fields, perfectly still, trying not to dwell on any one thing for too long lest I find a twisted version of it waiting for me upon waking.

Years later, I encountered something far worse than the malformed puppet of my father. It began when I, once again, wandered the endless landscape of my dreams. As I paced through a forest, I noticed a dark shadow pass in the periphery of my vision. Fearing it was my father, I followed to investigate.

I watched from behind a tree as a man cloaked in darkness entered a nearby clearing. No part of him was visible. Shadows trailed behind him like a long robe and the silhouette of a crown sat askew atop his head. He stood straight and proud. Power and authority hung about him much like the blackness in which he was shrouded.

The strangest aspect of this dark figure was the way he influenced the world around him. Everything near him became desaturated, its color drawn into the darkness of his core. His surroundings faded to a pale gray and succumbed to a sudden stillness, as if any semblance of life had been stolen from them. The things that passed out of his aura seemed altered, though in no discernable way. Something about them was simply wrong, like a drawing of a figure where the foreshortening is just slightly off.

I shifted my weight and a branch cracked beneath me. The dark figure whirled around and glared in my direction. Two glowing red orbs watched from beneath its crown. Terrified, I sprinted in the other direction. It gazed after me as I fled but made no move to follow.

I came across the dark figure many times after that. I called him the Gray King. Like my father, he followed me, though there was clear intent to his actions. He always watched closely, as if trying to figure something out. As time went on, he became increasingly present and his gaze grew more intense. He was studying me, though at the time I knew not why.

Then came the day where he did more than just watch. He approached me as I was relaxing in a meadow. He strode purposefully, his red eyes unwavering, fixated on me. I surged to my feet, prepared to run away. The Gray King's presence terrified me. I feared what might happen if I came within the radius of his strange aura.

However, before I could do anything, he was upon me. He grabbed my arm and I watched the darkness surge around him like innumerable black snakes clambering over his form. He fixed me with his piercing gaze and spoke at last.

"Let me out." His voice was deep and commanding, a suitable voice for a king.

"What?" I managed to say. His grip felt like ice on my arm and I trembled under the weight of his presence.

"I've watched you. You come and go as you please and take things as you like."

I tried to pull my arm away, but his grip was like iron. Despite yanking with all my might, his hold remained firm. "What do you mean?" I asked.

"You can take things from this world into the other. I've seen into you. I know what you did to your father."

I gasped at that. How could he have known about my father? That had happened years before and had remained a secret wholly my own.

"Take me to your world." The dark figure said. "I've remained imprisoned here for far too long. The time for your world's undoing is long past and my reckoning is at hand."

Even before he said it, I knew that bringing him to the waking world would wreak havoc. There was something wrong about the Gray King's presence. I felt myself affected by his aura. It felt like some substance deep inside me was coming undone, as if the very fabric that comprised me was being pulled apart and stitched into a creation of his own design.

"No," I said.

The King had no expression, but the shadows that enveloped him seemed to bristle and I could tell that he was angry.

"I will give you no choice." He said. He said it simply, not as a threat but rather a statement of fact. His voice sent shivers down my spine.

After that, he took me to a strange cavern in the forest. It felt as if I had no will of my own, and he dragged me behind him with titanic strength. He tortured me there. I won't go into details, but he did terrible things to me. You see, we were in the world of dreams where the laws of reality don't apply, and the limits of the body are exaggerated. As such, the amount of pain one can inflict is immeasurable.

I woke the next morning sweating and gasping for breath. I could still remember every excruciating moment I spent with that monster. I couldn't help but check my body for wounds, afraid that they too would follow me into the physical world. I found myself unharmed and was relieved that I had escaped the Gray King's grasp.

That night, as I went to bed, I expected to wake in a random place within the dream world. That's how it had always been. But upon falling asleep, I found myself back on his table, exactly where I'd been the night before. Once again, the torture resumed. Always with the same repeated phrase. *Bring me with you.*

I haven't slept in six days now. I've suffered his torture for too long. I dread closing my eyes for fear that I will open them and find myself once again upon his torture rack. The things he's done haunt me every waking moment, and I can no longer tear my mind away from him. Sleep is overtaking me once again.

I'm sorry. Countless tortures have made me his creature. I'm beginning to realize that this is his world. It always has been. The world of dreams is merely a prison. When he returns, this reality will be his to rule or destroy as he wills. I tried my hardest. I'm sorry. I fear he will be here when I wake next.

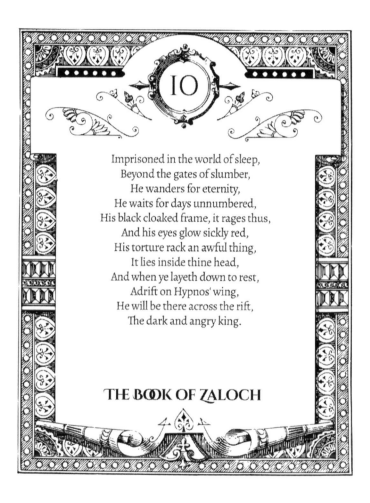

IO

Imprisoned in the world of sleep,
Beyond the gates of slumber,
He wanders for eternity,
He waits for days unnumbered,
His black cloaked frame, it rages thus,
And his eyes glow sickly red,
His torture rack an awful thing,
It lies inside thine head,
And when ye layeth down to rest,
Adrift on Hypnos' wing,
He will be there across the rift,
The dark and angry king.

THE BOOK OF ZALOCH

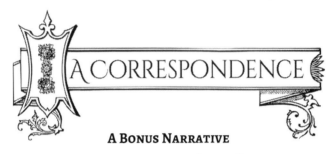

A BONUS NARRATIVE

IN COLLABORATION WITH JACOB ROMINES

AS DOCTOR MURKWELL

INCLUDING HINTS OF HIS COLLECTION,

SOMETHING OTHER

Doctor Murkwell,

I've read much of your research regarding the existence of conscious beings that lie beyond humanity's current grasp of natural science as well as papers you've published discussing modern advances in the study of parapsychology and its legitimacy. While many may deride your work as fantastical, I find you to be one of the most studious and empirically thorough researchers of abnormal phenomena still living. Your work with the Princeton Engineering Anomalies Research Program is some of the most convincing and thought-provoking I've ever come across. You seem to be acutely aware of the existence of things beyond our wildest dreams, and, rather than letting these beliefs dwindle as mere superstition, you work to prove and understand those things which dwell at the fringes of our reality.

It is for these aforementioned reasons that I come to you, and only you, with an unusual theory. I hope that you will consider it more seriously than my contemporaries. I myself study anomalies, though I do so somewhat differently. I earned my Ph.D. in ancient literature at Columbia and spent many years delving into the most esoteric and strange works that I could get my hands on. In doing so, I found many descriptions of beings beyond science, and, after devouring so many ancient writings, I began to see commonalities among the myriad descriptions scattered throughout history. These entities became my obsession, and I began to research them with fervor. Upon doing so, I've come to a startling conclusion.

However, before continuing, I must first ask you a question. Have you ever heard of the Book of Zaloch? You may otherwise know it as The Book of Zaloch the Mad or, more obscurely, Prophecies from the Mad Mountains. It is an ancient and little-known piece of literature and has lost much of its significance in academic circles within the past century. However, I hope that you may have some familiarity with it, as it has long been associated with the arcane and occult.

Thank you for your time, and I look forward to your response.

Best Regards,
Doctor Orwell Pengloss
October 30th, 2011

***

Dr. Pengloss,

I am pleased to hear from you. I must apologize for the time it has taken me to respond. I am currently at work on an extensive personal investigation, and it threatens to consume me entirely. Regardless, I'm interested in hearing your theory, though I profess that I lack more than a cursory familiarity with ancient literature. I'm aware of several religions that coincide with my theories, some of which are extremely archaic - but this "Book of Zaloch" is too obscure for me. Note that my specialties lie in the natural sciences, and my knowledge of mythology, philosophy, and other dimensions of the humanities was acquired to provide background to the oddities I've found in the material world. However, I do not intend to dismiss your fields of study - perhaps, if my current research ends satisfactorily, I will find the time to review your other writings.

In the meantime, I would appreciate an articulation of your theory. Especially considering that you found it so related to my body of work that you tracked down my current address - not an easy thing to do, considering the steps I have taken to ensure my reclusion.

Regards,
A. Murkwell
December 21st, 2011

***

Doctor Murkwell,

Thank you for responding to my message and worry not about the delay. I understand that you are a busy man, and I appreciate you taking the time to entertain my theories. I'm glad that you have at least a passing familiarity with ancient literature, as that is more than I can expect from most. However, I fear I may need to do some explaining in light of your unfamiliarity with The Book of Zaloch.

The Book of Zaloch is perhaps one of the most ancient pieces of writing in existence. It's a series of hundreds of poems (cantos) carved into clay tablets dated to nearly 5,000 years ago, rivaling the most ancient examples of written language. A large cache of them was found in Babylon, though many have been lost over the years. There is little known about the author other than the fact that his name is something roughly along the lines of Zaloch, sometimes with the epithet "the mad." It seems stories about this Zaloch were passed down orally as a sort of folktale in Mesopotamia. These folktales describe him as a mad prophet who lived in the mountains and saw all possible futures and all possible worlds. The translations are rough, but it's possible that this may represent the first-ever example of a multiverse theory.

I'm sure by now that you're wondering how this connects to your work. Please bear with me a little longer, and I will explain. You see, the cantos were intended to be prophetic in nature. They were poetic descriptions of Zaloch's visions. However, they were never taken seriously, and he was thought to be mad. Religious cults centered around The Book of Zaloch have sprung up a few times in history. However, within recent centuries the text has faded largely into obscurity.

I only stumbled across The Book of Zaloch by chance when it appeared as a small footnote in a textbook on ancient literature. Intrigued, I tracked down the nearest available translation and found myself enamored with the work. I began to study it intently, finding every possible translation, every minute difference in syntax and verbiage. It was at this time that I began to notice correlations between the things Zaloch spoke of and entities referenced in other ancient works. The number of these entities which existed in other works went beyond coincidence, and there is even more evidence of the book's prophetic nature. For example, it depends upon which translation you use, but it is highly likely that Zaloch referenced the great tree Yggdrasil long before Norse mythology came into being. Other references like this exist in the Book of Zaloch, and it seems as if they can only be understood in the context of future events.

You see, Zaloch's cantos construct a basic mythology. From what I can gather, it describes some ancient god or creator who went mad and shattered into an infinite number of pieces. This great shattering caused the universe to also shatter into a number of different realities. Once again, we see an early incarnation of the multiverse theory. These shattered pieces of the god, often called The Shattered God, seem to have become smaller, less powerful gods and entities. The cantos describe them and how they inhabit our reality.

This leads us to my theory. Zaloch states that the universe was shattered into a number of parallel realities. However, the broken aspects of the Creator are not subject to the limitations of dimensional space as we are. Therefore, each piece can only exist in one of infinite realities. The cantos references entities that are the head and heart of the Shattered God, which surely are central aspects of his existence. Further reading of the cantos indicates that the other aspects are drawn by these integral pieces.

Consequently, I have come to a horrifying conclusion. Both the head and the heart of the Shattered God exist in our reality and no other. His other parts are slowly being drawn by them, coming together into a central place: our world. Think of the multiverse as a great column of water, each infinitely small cross-section representing a different reality. This column has been stirred so that particulates (the Shattered God's aspects) float about it randomly. Our world rests at the bottom of this column, and these particulates are slowly settling down and becoming part of our world.

I'm afraid that we live in the worst of all possible worlds, the gutter of the multiverse, a terrible reality in which things will only degrade and become more monstrous as these demented creatures seep through the cracks between universes. Even now, I wouldn't be surprised if there were an increase in reports of paranormal phenomena as a result of these new entities. We live in terrifying times, Doctor Murkwell. I fear for what our world will become.

Best Regards,
Doctor Orwell Pengloss
December 27th, 2011

***

Dr. Pengloss,

While I am quite interested in this theory of yours, and am not one to dismiss an idea based solely on its fantastic qualities, I must first ask: do you have any empirical evidence for this? Any experimental data? Observed, documented, and studied phenomena? If not, I must correct your use of the word "theory" to mean hypothesis. While anecdotes can lead to fascinating information, I must stress that the role of unprovable, secondhand accounts should be taken as suggestive of more testable phenomena, which should *then* lead to an overall theory informed by evidence.

Furthermore, what suggests that Zaloch possessed any deeper ontological knowledge whatsoever? Many disparate mythologies are known to converge on each other; to me, this trend is only notable when they also converge on scientific work. Keep in mind, humans are strange creatures, and esoteric minds exist in every society. It is very possible this "Zaloch" man was in the thrall of a madness of an entirely human origin. That said, I have encountered evidence of human consciousness appearing to be "contacted" or influenced by extraneous forces, so I am willing to grant the possibility of an extraordinary insight - which you or other theologically-inclined people may understand as "divine".

But I take issue with this terminology, and the larger religious narrative you have constructed. Personally, I believe that there are many entities throughout the world beyond the limits of human capacities - this we can agree upon. But why must they be aspects of a central being? I propose that these beings arose through natural processes, even though the beings themselves appear supernatural since their mechanisms of creation, operation, and sustenance are outside the needle's-eye of human understanding. A conscious being that split into many others? What's more, this conscious being was the creator of the universe? A chilling thought, but I abide by a more naturalistic understanding. Fundamentally, I consider myself an empiricist, though my struggle consists of trying to find the limits and loopholes of human senses. Mythology tends to assign grand narratives to the unknown. But what is known is determined by the scope of our brain! Most are familiar with my parapsychological work, but as a young man, I specialized in evolutionary biology, and it is that perspective that has allowed me to glimpse the shadows moving in the murk beyond our minds.

As such, I am hesitant to view your Shattered God theory as more than an unnerving explanation for unnerving yet disparate phenomena. You seem a learned man, but I urge you not to delve too deep into the enticing worlds of metanarratives and mythologies. These things can blind the brain even further, and I have spent my entire life realizing just how blind the brain already is.

Sincerely,
A. Murkwell
February 27th, 2012

***

Doctor Murkwell,

I understand your perspective on this, and I also understand that, as men from differing backgrounds, we synthesize the information available to us differently. However, in reports of interactions with supernatural entities, it is not uncommon for people who have spoken with said entities to report the creature mentioning something greater than themselves of which they are a part. While there are other ways to interpret this finding, it would not be difficult to understand these references in the context of my "hypothesis," as you put it.

Additionally, there are many historical references to a broken or mad creator, or descriptions of gods coming into existence from the parts of greater gods. For example, Aphrodite is said to have been born from the severed genitals of Uranus. In the *Bhagavad Gita*, Vishnu's body is described as comprising the universe and his body parts representing different things. We even see a similar thought process in Catholicism, where the different aspects of the church are thought of as part of the body of Christ. For example, we might look at 1 Corinthians 12:12, "*The body is a unit, though it is comprised of many parts. And although its parts are many, they all form one body. So it is with Christ.*" If this isn't enough, see Colossians 1:18, "*And He is the head of the body, the church; He is the beginning and firstborn from among the dead, so that in all things He may have preeminence*."

Is it not possible that these are all conceptions of the same creator being? Do these not all sound like different ways of describing the Shattered God? When so many mythologies that are formulated independently - separated physically, culturally, and temporally - all describe such similar interpretations of their deities, how can we not lend this idea some credence?

I am not myself a religious man, but, given the countless correlating descriptions of deities across numerous cultures, how can I not believe in something greater than the biological? You yourself, by your interest in parapsychology, admit that there are things and forces beyond human understanding. When I say gods and deities, I do not mean so in a religious sense. I only mean that they possess power beyond our wildest dreams or capabilities and exist on a slightly altered plane.

I may not have numbers for you to fiddle with or some dead simian creature for you to dissect, but there is no denying that the things I've described seem to point to a greater whole, something beyond comprehension or hope. We live in dark times, Doctor Murkwell, and they are only getting darker. While people may cite declining morals or the internet as causes for this darkness, I know that there are strings being pulled behind the scenes by twisted hands with capacities that would make you tremble. Things will only become worse from here on out. His parts are coming together and something darker is assembling.

Regards,
Doctor Orwell Pengloss
March 1st, 2012

***

Dr. Pengloss,

Forgive my letter-writing pace. Oftentimes, I forget the rest of reality exists when I am engrossed in my current preoccupation.

For the sake of mutual respect between those who are willing to gaze into the abyss, I will suspend my judgement on this hypothesis - which you appear to have thrown the full weight of your belief behind - and resign myself to a congratulations on the depth of your study. I wish I could discuss this with you in person, for working together, it is possible that we might indeed unravel some terrible secret. In addition, for the sake of scholarly opposition, I was more emphatic in my earlier letters regarding the role of religion in the discovery of the abnormal.

I have also encountered a religion which has influenced the scope of my research, though it does not appear to have the same depth of literary tradition as your "Shattered God." Throughout history, there appear to be small sects and even isolated individuals who worship... well, I'm hesitant to use the word biology. Perhaps it would be apt to say they worship a being which represents unchecked life itself, which represents biology in all its power - producer, predator, parasite, scavenger. This religion has not been given a name by the historical community, seeing as I am the only scholar who has ever put the pieces together, linking the similarities between groups as disparate as ancient fertile-crescent farmers and a group of disturbed craftsmen in 1800's Maine.

But this religion has never been my primary focus, and right now, I am engaged in a project of an apparently unconnected nature. I am hesitant to share details regarding my current study, only to explain to you that it is *proven* to be very dangerous and I am unsure whether I will see my research through to the end. Does your theory incorporate anything regarding a malevolent and possibly-living structure? As in, a being that constitutes a physical location? A term that is often misapplied to such a concept is "genius loci." Have you done any reading or research on such beings?

Regards,
A. Murkwell
September 19th, 2012

***

Doctor Murkwell,

Regarding your last question, it is entirely possible that a malevolent physical structure exists as an aspect of the Shattered God. Parts of The Book of Zaloch may even reference entire sentient environments, depending on the translation. The sources I've researched are rife with descriptions of entities which I'm sure pertain to your work. I believe these creatures to also be aspects of the Shattered God or servants of said aspects.

I'm glad that you are willing to work with me and my research; however, I can't help but sense some hesitancy on your part. I don't blame you for this, as my ideas are surely unusual. Additionally, I have not been completely honest with you. I was reluctant to tell you at first, but I now trust that I won't be dismissed outright.

I have personally had an experience with an aspect of the Shattered God. More specifically, I believe that I have encountered an entity that corresponds to his head. I believe this experience will appeal more to your empirical senses. However, I am hesitant to discuss the details through something as indiscrete as a letter. If word of this were to ever get out, my standing with employers and colleagues would be severely jeopardized. If you would like to meet in person, I would be more than happy to relate this frankly terrifying experience to you. Please respond in a timely fashion. I fear this experience has tainted me in a way. I am marked by Him. I need any help I can get.

Best Regards,
Doctor Orwell Pengloss
September 23rd, 2012

***

Doctor Murkwell,

I realize that you're a busy man, but I beg of you to respond. You yourself have admitted that my ideas deserve some merit, and I only have further proof if we could just meet in person. I feel that I've been changing. It's as if I'm standing on the edge of some soaring, precarious cliff and the turbulent waters of arcane knowledge are splashing below me. My eyes are being opened to something, Doctor Murkwell. I need your assistance.

Please reply at your earliest convenience.

Best Regards,
Doctor Orwell Pengloss
October 31st, 2012

***

Orwell I am entrusting you with the possibility of receiving my work should I perish. I am going to do something enormously foolish in the name of science and I am sorry that I cannot help you at the moment. Know that in my isolation I have appreciated your correspondence more than I may have let on and I consider you a worthy scholar. If you receive another letter from me it will be a triumph of enormous magnitude.

Sincerely,
Aaron Murkwell
December 1st, 2012

THE END

A NOTE FROM THE AUTHOR

Things Undone is a myriad of firsts. It is my first collection of prose work, my first attempt at writing short stories with any seriousness, and my first venture into the world of weird fiction and cosmic horror. It was during the writing of this book that I truly began to feel a sense of style. I felt my skills sharpen, and I can honestly say I am proud of this book. I hope that you feel as good about reading Things Undone as I do about having written it.

Regardless, this is still the work of a twenty-year-old. I penned this while juggling classes, work, and familial obligations. It may not be the best, but I am confident in the quality of this book. Furthermore, I feel this is the first step on what I hope to be a long and successful journey. I have always enjoyed horror, but it was through writing this that I truly fell in love with the genre. I plan on improving my storytelling abilities so that I may write even better works in the future, both for myself and for you, the reader.

I plan on continuing to write within The Shattered God Mythos. It is my vision that it become a grand, sprawling world of terror and fantasy with numerous interconnected stories. I hope I have done well in introducing you to my world. I plan on turning it into a rich mythological system, and I hope that you find it both entertaining and intriguing.

Lastly, I want to thank you for reading my work. The fact that you've even read this far means the world to me. Nothing makes me happier than watching someone fall in love with one of my stories. Your support is everything. If you enjoyed the book, please leave a review on Amazon. I'd love to hear your thoughts!

ACKNOWLEDGEMENTS

Jacob Romines,

If there is anyone who inspired me to write this, it is you. Through reading your horror stories (and fueling the competitive flames which have kept us at each other's throats for the past seven years), I found the inspiration to begin writing this. You have helped me at every step of the way, from conception to execution to editing. Your help and support have been invaluable, and I look forward to our continued love, support, and friendship in the future.

(Jacob also writes in the genre of weird fiction. His book, **Something Other**, is absolutely incredible and first inspired me to begin writing this. Check it out on Amazon if you want another good horror read and if you'd like to read more about Dr. Murkwell.)

Lilly Weakley,

Your encouragement and support throughout this arduous process has meant the world to me. You have always been there for me. You helped me get through these stories, but – more importantly – you helped me get through life for these past few months. You have always been my rock and my place of refuge in the most tumultuous of times. I love you forever.

Kyle Romines,

Your advice, editing, encouragement, and discussion have helped me immensely in the writing of this book. You write both well and prolifically, and you have been a great source of inspiration for me. Furthermore, you have motivated me to write better in the hopes that you will be impressed. I am forever grateful for your help.

(Kyle is a writer with too many books to list. Look him up on Amazon to check out all of his wonderful stories.)

Ronan Kinsella,

Your friendship kept me sane while I was writing this. I can always relax and joke around with you. The crushing and eternal weight of the world seems a little less heavy when you're around. You're my brother and I love you.

Sarah Littlehale,

Your support and enthusiasm for my work has made the writing and completion of this book both easier and more satisfying than I could have imagined. My thanks is yours forever.

H.P. Lovecraft, Thomas Ligotti, Mearle Prout, Laird Barron, S.T. Joshi, Stephen King, Neil Gaiman, Junji Ito

To you, my highest respects. If it were not for your efforts, the world of horror would be very different and likely would not exist in the capacity that it does today. Your work has kept me entertained, day and night, from childhood to now. It is through your writing that I have been introduced to the world of horror, and I am forever grateful for this weird and twisted world of ours.

Other Books by Travis Liebert

Things Undone: A Collection of Horror Stories

Things Unknown: A Collection of Horror Stories

The Anomaly Archives: Stories of Supernatural Misfortune and Horror

Badwater: A Horror Story

This is Death, Love, Life: A Collection of Poetry

Perchance to Dream: : A Collection of Poetry

Everything in Between: : A Collection of Poetry

ABOUT THE AUTHOR

Travis Liebert is a 20-year-old Junior at the University of Louisville and is currently pursuing a degree in psychology. He has a variety of interests including writing, art, music, fashion, and acting like an idiot whenever possible. One thing he particularly dislikes is writing about himself in the third person to avoid sounding pretentious.

He has been a voracious reader ever since he was a child and could reliably be found devouring Stephen King books by the time he was eleven. He began writing at a young age, but never did so with any seriousness or consistency until he was eighteen. *Things Undone* is the first comprehensive work of prose fiction that he has ever written. However, he has previously published three poetry collections that are available on Amazon.

His Instagram, Tumblr, Twitter, and (regrettably) TikTok usernames are all @travisliebert. His website is **travisliebert.com** and you can find his facebook page at **facebook.com/authortravisliebert**. Feel free to contact him at travismliebert@gmail.com.

Printed in Great Britain
by Amazon

45645148R10111